'I somehow get the feeling you're not going to be too good for my blood pressure whenever we're around one another.'

She had a vague suspicion that could work both ways. 'Well, I'm sorry about that,' she murmured, 'but I'm sure you'll manage somehow.' She liked him, but she wasn't going to respond to his flirting.

She couldn't. Her time with Ewan had taught her that flirtation could get out of hand and lead to some heavy involvement, and before you knew it you were embroiled in a situation that was bounding out of control. She couldn't go through that again.

She gave him a sympathetic glance. 'Some people say a cold shower does the trick.'

He gave a rueful laugh. 'You're not going to take pity on me, are you? I had in mind a much more romantic prescription.'

Dear Reader

There's something really special about college days, with young people so full of energy and sparkle, living life to the full. Everything takes on the brightest colours. Their lives are filled with music, deep, lasting friendships and the sheer joy of being alive and trying new things.

So when the four young people in my book get together to share a house things are bound to fizz. It isn't long before Ben and Jade find themselves drawn to one another—things are definitely beginning to warm up— but, as always, there are pitfalls along the way.

Jade is getting over a broken relationship, and the last thing she needs is to find herself falling for Ben. It's just not going to happen—is it?

With love

Joanna

 **ISLINGTON**

Please return this item on or before the last date stamped below or you may be liable to overdue charges. To renew an item call the number below, or access the online catalogue at www.islington.gov.uk/libraries. You will need your library membership number and PIN number.

2 7 JUL 2015		

Islington Libraries

020 7527 6900   **www.islington.gov.uk/libraries**

DR LANGLEY: PROTECTOR OR PLAYBOY?

BY
JOANNA NEIL

First published in Great Britain 2012
by Mills & Boon, an imprint of Harlequin (UK) Limited.
Harlequin (UK) Limited, Eton House, 18-24 Paradise Road,
Richmond, Surrey TW9 1SR

© Joanna Neil 2012

ISBN: 978 0 263 22856 4

Harlequin (UK) policy is to use papers that are natural, renewable
and recyclable products and made from wood grown in sustainable
forests. The logging and manufacturing process conform to the
legal environmental regulations of the country of origin.

Printed and bound in Great Britain
by CPI Antony Rowe, Chippenham, Wiltshire

When **Joanna Neil** discovered Mills & Boon®, her lifelong addiction to reading crystallised into an exciting new career writing Medical™ Romance. Her characters are probably the outcome of her varied lifestyle, which includes working as a clerk, typist, nurse and infant teacher. She enjoys dressmaking and cooking at her Leicestershire home. Her family includes a husband, son and daughter, an exuberant yellow Labrador and two slightly crazed cockatiels. She currently works with a team of tutors at her local education centre to provide creative writing workshops for people interested in exploring their own writing ambitions.

Recent titles by the same author:

A COTSWOLD CHRISTMAS BRIDE
THE TAMING OF DR ALEX DRAYCOTT
BECOMING DR BELLINI'S BRIDE
PLAYBOY UNDER THE MISTLETOE

These books are also available in eBook format from www.millsandboon.co.uk

CHAPTER ONE

'I DON'T know how you can face coming here straight after putting in a full day's work at the hospital.' Matt Berenger glanced briefly at Jade before removing the filter from his coffee cup and putting it to one side. He began to spoon sugar into the hot liquid. 'I need a break before I can even think about starting on anything else.'

'Put it down to sheer necessity,' Jade answered with a rueful smile. 'I need to keep my student loan down to the minimum.' She sent a fleeting glance around the room. All the customers appeared to be content for the moment and it seemed no one needed her attention, so there was probably no harm in spending a moment or two swapping news with Matt.

She rested her empty tray on her hip, and briefly tugged at the skirt of her waitress uniform with her free hand. 'This outfit drives me mad,' she muttered through her teeth. 'It's totally the wrong size for me and it's forever riding up.'

Matt studied her, his dark head tilted to one side. 'Looks okay to me.'

Jade made a wry face. Did he know anything at all about the way women's clothes should fit?

He tested the coffee for heat and then took a sip. 'So how was your first day in Paediatrics?'

'It was okay, I suppose.' She frowned. 'There's so much to remember, where everything's kept, for a start—lab forms, equipment, linen—and then there are all the new people you meet. The consultant, the registrar, the rest of the team, and nurses,—and that's without even mentioning the patients...' Her green eyes closed briefly. 'To see those young children looking so poorly just breaks my heart.'

She pulled in a quick breath. 'But at least there was someone there who was nearer to my level—he's a year ahead of me, though, like you—he's a pre-registration doctor, doing his year-one foundation course. I think perhaps he's a few years older than me, so maybe he was involved in something else before he set out to study medicine.' She frowned. 'In fact, you probably know him, if he's in the same year group as you. Ben Langley? Does that ring a bell?'

'Ben.' Matt nodded, his mouth curving. 'Oh yes. We've been together on quite a few placements, and in lectures, of course. He's okay—I like him. And I think you'll find he's extremely popular with all the females for miles around.' He swallowed more coffee. 'He seems to know his way around the hospital system, and he's very amenable. I'm sure if you ask him, he'll help you out with anything you need to know.'

'Yes, I guess so. I did turn to him a couple of times, since he looked as though he had the situation in hand, but I didn't want to do it too often for fear of looking as though I was completely hopeless.' She gave a small sigh. 'It's just that everyone seems to know so much more than me. They're all so confident, so capable, whereas I was wandering around feeling lost most of the time. Did you feel that way when you were in your fifth year? I'd expected to find things a bit easier by now.'

'We all go through it.' Matt smiled. 'Anyway, as far as I can see, you've been doing really well. Just think, this time next year you'll be in the same position as me, a foundation-year doctor.'

She gave a soft sigh, trying to imagine it. 'I can't wait.'

'Oh, so you can't wait, eh?' a sharp voice snarled in her ear, making her jump. 'But you think the customers can? *Alors*! You should be waiting tables, *n'est ce pas?* Let us have no more of this chit-chat. *Allez!*'

'Uh… Oh—I'm sorry.' Jade straightened up and shot a look at her boss, Jacques. He was an excitable man in his middle years, slightly overweight, with brown hair that was all over the place from his habit of running a hand through it. He was given to short bursts of irritability, and she guessed that came from the responsibility that went along with running a café bar in the middle of London. Today was a bad day, because the air-conditioning had broken down and the temperature in the kitchen was almost too much to bear.

She gave Matt an apologetic smile. 'I should get on,' she murmured. 'I'll see you later, back at the house, and perhaps you can tell me all about how you got on in A and E.'

'Will do.' Matt drank his coffee, tilting back his head

and draining every last drop. 'I'd better head off, anyway. I don't suppose Lucy will have given a thought to getting anything in for supper. Her head's in the clouds these days.'

Jade leapt to her friend's defence. 'It's not her fault, you know. She has a lot on her mind.'

'Don't we all?'

Matt left the café and Jade concentrated on clearing tables. Her boss obviously didn't like to see her standing around talking to the customers but, as far as she could see, no new people had come in off the street.

No sooner had that thought crossed her mind than the main door swung open and a group of men entered. There were four of them, all smartly dressed in suits, shirts and ties, and one of them was the very man she'd just been talking about, Ben Langley.

He walked towards an empty table and sat down. On the wards, he gave the impression he was someone you could rely on. And here he was no different. He had that look of a man who was totally at ease with himself and everything around him…calm, yet purposeful.

She studied him surreptitiously as she waited for the group to settle down. A head taller than she was, he had dark hair and features that somehow compelled you to look, and look again. His eyes, she recalled, were a pleasing mix of grey and blue, and he had a way of looking at you that made it seem that you had his full attention.

And he was looking at her right now. She gave a faint start, her cheeks flushing with heat because he had caught her out, watching him.

His gaze was fixed on her, and she gave herself a mental shake. Get a grip, she chided herself inwardly. He was just looking at her because he wanted to order some food, and she was the waitress, for heaven's sake.

He smiled as she walked over to the table. He had a naturally warm and friendly manner that automatically drew everyone in. She'd been aware of it from the start, and it had been fairly obvious that all the nurses had fallen for him straight away. Then again, the number-one rule for junior doctors was for them to make friends with the nursing staff if they were to make any headway in the job, and he had managed that for sure.

She drew in a deep breath. It was highly embarrassing that he and his friends should find her working here, of all places—in an instant her street cred had gone right through the floor.

'Hello. What can I get for you?' she asked. She gave them all a welcoming smile and let her glance roam fleetingly over his friends.

'Steak burger and fries for me,' the fair-haired one said. 'I'm starving.' He checked out her long, chestnut-coloured hair and gave her an appreciative smile.

'I'll have the toasted cheese sandwich,' the young man sitting next to him said. 'No expense spared, you see,' he added in mock humour. 'We're celebrating our first day in new placements—at the hospital across the way,' he added by way of explanation.

She nodded, but Ben said softly, 'She knows all about placements, Jack. She's one of us.'

Jack's eyes widened. 'Really? How come I've not seen you around?'

'We're in different year groups, perhaps?' She gave a light shrug and concentrated on writing down the orders.

'Maybe you can tell us what you've been up to so far this year,' Jack said in a musing tone. 'We could swap notes. It's always good to have some insight into other specialties. I started on the renal unit today.'

'Jade's a fifth-year student,' Ben explained, and she glanced at him. He remembered her name? It didn't mean anything, of course. Perhaps he was good at that sort of thing. She'd remembered his name because he was the kind of man you didn't forget.

'That's right,' she murmured, adding for the benefit of the rest of the group, 'I started in Paediatrics today, alongside Ben. I'd really like to stay and swap notes, but unfortunately I'm already in trouble with my boss for standing around talking.' She pulled a face. 'I can feel him glaring at me from the kitchen.'

'Oh, dear.' Ben acknowledged that with a sympathetic smile. 'Then we'd better hurry up and decide what we want to eat.' He studied the menu along with his other friend and gave her their order a moment or two later.

Jade tucked her notepad into her pocket and walked over to the kitchen. She hoped Ben wasn't following her progress. The wretched uniform was sliding up over her hips again and it took all her willpower to resist the urge to tug it back down.

'Here we are,' she said a short time later, setting down the plates of food. 'Burger and fries, toasted cheese sandwich, baguette and crepes. I'll bring your drinks along in a minute or two.'

'Thanks.' Ben accepted the plate of savoury crepes she put before him. His friends began to tuck in, chatting to one another, while Ben put his food to one side for the moment and looked at her. 'It's good to see you again,' he murmured, letting his gaze drift over her and making her suddenly conscious of the way her skirt clung to her and of the hint of cleavage displayed by the cotton top of the uniform. 'I expect we'll soon get used to working alongside one another. The first day in a placement is always a bit unnerving, isn't it? But you seemed to be coping well enough.'

'Did I?' She gave a soft laugh. 'I suppose it was okay once I managed to spend time with the patients. Everything else seemed to fade into the background then. Apart from when the consultant came to do his rounds. That was a bit scary.' She looked at him, a small frown in her green eyes. She doubted he had any such problems.

At the end of his working day he seemed perfectly relaxed. He had removed his jacket, and where he had rolled back his shirtsleeves she saw that his strong forearms were lightly bronzed, covered with a smattering of dark hair.

'He put you on the spot a bit, didn't he, asking about the baby's stridor?' His voice was deep and low, smoothing over her like comforting hot chocolate. 'I thought it was a bit unfair of him, really, to do that to you on your first day.'

She nodded. 'You're right. His questions left me

flummoxed for a while, I must say. To begin with, I wondered if the strange noises the baby was making when he breathed in were to do with a respiratory problem, but at least I did get it together enough to suggest that we should check out his throat as well as his chest.'

'And that was the right thing to say, as things turned out.' He smiled, a full-on smile that curved his well-shaped mouth and glimmered in the depths of those smoky, grey-blue eyes. Caught unawares, Jade's heart did a funny little flip-over in the middle of her chest.

'Yes.' Her voice was husky. What on earth was the matter with her? She hadn't reacted this way to any man since she'd met Ewan. And her experience with him had surely been enough to warn her to keep her emotions under control.

She brought her mind back to the baby at the hospital. She'd learned that the infant was struggling with a 'soft' larynx, a condition where the immature cartilage folded inwards on inhalation, causing an airway obstruction.

'I guess so,' she said. 'It's a shame the baby's ill enough to need surgery, though. He's only six months old—I'd hate it if a child of mine needed an operation at such a young age.'

'Me, too.'

Out of the corner of her eye, she saw her boss beginning to glower at her from the kitchen once more, and she quietly excused herself. More customers were coming in, and she and the rest of the staff were kept busy for the next half-hour, seeing to their needs.

There was no time for a breather. As customers ate

up and left the café, Jade cleared away the dishes and wiped the tables clean. Now her tray was filled with pudding bowls, cups and saucers, and as she headed back towards the kitchen with them, she saw that Ben and his friends were preparing to leave. They nodded towards her and she returned the gesture.

She wasn't quite sure what happened next. One moment she was treading carefully between the tables, glancing at the customers to see who might shortly need attention, and the next her foot had shot out from under her and she began to tumble backwards. The tray wobbled precariously and she desperately tried to keep it aloft while fighting to keep her balance, but all the time she knew it was going to be a losing battle. Her heart sank as crockery began to slide off the tray, heading for the floor. It would only be a matter of seconds before she would follow.

Then, as she resigned herself to her fate, she discovered that strong arms were holding her, effortlessly taking her weight and steadying her.

'You're okay, I have you,' Ben said. His tone was reassuring, supportive, washing over her like a soothing balm. He helped her to regain her balance, and even as she tried to thank him, she was unhappily aware of the tableware hitting the floor tiles with a resounding crash. A small cheer went up from the diners close by.

'Que se passe-t-il? Qu'avez vous fait?'

Jade groaned as her boss hurried towards her. His dark brows pulled together, meeting in a scowl.

'I… It was an accident,' she told him in dismay. 'I don't know how it happened.' All the time she was aware of Ben's nearness, of his hand on her elbow and the warmth of his touch coursing through her body and setting her nerves alight. For the second time that evening, her cheeks were flushed with heat. Was she bound to constantly make a fool of herself around him?

'Zut!' Jacques was not pleased. 'It is a mess.'

'Yes. Yes, it is. I'll clean it up,' Jade promised. 'I'm sorry.'

'I am sorry, too. *C'est vrai.*' He glowered at her.

Her ankle was stinging, and she looked down to see that a jagged piece of broken plate had cut into her, slashing the flesh. Blood seeped from the gash.

'You're hurt,' Ben said, pulling in a sharp breath. 'That wound needs dressing.' He frowned. 'Perhaps you should be taking the management to task, instead of the other way round. After all, it wasn't your fault that someone spilled ice cream on the floor—in fact, in the circumstances you might have been badly hurt.'

'Is that what it was? No... I'm.... It...' She broke off as Ben's fingers gave a warning squeeze on her arm.

Her boss flinched. 'That's it, of course.' He hit his palm against his forehead and looked around. 'I see now what's to be done. You should go home,' he said, coming to a sudden decision. 'Take the rest of the night off.'

'But I... I'm sure I'll be fine... And anyway I can't go home...I have to work. I need to work.'

His expression was pained. 'Uh...with pay, *naturellement*,' he muttered under his breath, as though the words had to be torn out of him. 'Anyway, you're not far off the end of your shift. Just go, and we will forget all this. Now. *Allez!*'

'But I...' Her protests were cut off as Ben firmly turned her away and urged her towards a door marked 'Staff Only'.

'You should go and get changed. But before you do that, find a first-aid box and cover that wound—unless it's going to be awkward for you. Would you like me to help you with it?'

She shook her head. 'No, that's okay... I can manage, thanks.'

'All right, then go and get your bag, or whatever.' He gave her a light push from behind.

'I will.' She was aware of the other men waiting by the main door, and her chagrin was complete now that all of his friends had witnessed her stumble. Not only was she a waitress, she was a clumsy one into the bargain.

She gazed at him full on. 'Thanks again for your help.' She risked one last quick glance back to where she had slipped, and saw that Jacques had grabbed a brush and dustpan and was clearing up the broken crockery. Ever the showman, he gazed at the people who were looking on. 'I am good to my staff, see? That one—she is a medical student.' He inclined his head in Jade's direction. 'Who knows—I may find that I need her help one day.' He grinned.

Jade came out of the rest room a few minutes later. She had changed into jeans and T-shirt, and put on a light jacket in case the spring evening had turned chilly.

Looking around, she was startled to find Ben waiting for her in the lounge area.

'I didn't really expect you to hang around,' she said, her green eyes thoughtful. 'What about your friends? Shouldn't you be with them?'

He shook his head. 'I sent them on ahead, but I dare say I'll meet up with them later. For now, I'd much rather be with you—I wanted to make sure that you weren't too shaken up. That was a nasty cut.'

'I'm all right, thanks to you.' She smiled. 'You did a great job of catching me.' She glanced up at him as they went out of the main door and on to the street. 'You really don't need to stay with me, you know. I'll be fine.'

'I do know, but I will, all the same.' He looked around. 'How do you get to and from the hospital? Do you go by bus, or do you use the tube?'

'The bus, usually, or if it's a pleasant day and I have plenty of time, I walk. I enjoy the fresh air and the exercise. I live just a mile or so from here.'

He nodded. 'Which would you prefer to do now— walk, or take the bus?'

'I think I'd rather walk, as it's a pleasant evening.'

'Are you sure? Isn't your ankle going to give you problems if you do that?'

'No, it's fine, thanks.' She'd washed it and covered the area with a dressing, and though it was still sore, it would be okay.

'Good. I'll walk you home.'

She was quiet for a moment or two, but then she said, 'Okay. Thanks.' There didn't seem much point in protesting any more. He'd made up his mind, and maybe, for whatever reason, he felt that she needed to be watched over.

The sun was setting as they walked along the street that was made up of bars and coffee shops. At this time of the evening it was fairly noisy, with music filtering through open doors and windows, and with boisterous young people intent on having a good time.

'How often do you have to work at the café?' Ben asked. He was frowning. 'Do you have to put in a lot of hours?'

'It's a fairly flexible arrangement,' she told him. 'Jacques appears to be a bit uptight, but he's not a bad employer, really. He's just having a bad day. He knows how I'm fixed, and he's fairly accommodating. I generally help out on evenings when they're particularly busy, and I do half a dozen or so hours at the weekends when I can pull them in.'

He shook his head. 'It can't be easy. It's a shame you have to take a part time job while you're at medical school. Training to be a doctor is not exactly an easy option, and there's a tremendous amount of studying to be fitted in. It can't be good for you, burning the candle at both ends. It must be a worry, making sure that you stay on top form.'

His comments stirred her own fears and she turned to him with a concerned expression. 'Do you think I'm not up to it? Does it look that way? I've always done my best, and I'd hoped I managed fairly well at the hospital today. Of course, the consultant's opinion is another matter. But, then, he was out to make a point, to put me on the spot and let me know that I have to be on my toes and bone up on the kinds of situations that will come my way.'

He looked into her eyes, recognising her insecurity, and his glance warmed her. 'I thought you did remarkably well. But you're not stressed out with exams right now. How will you cope when the pressure's on towards the end of next month?'

She gave a light shrug. 'I'll cope the same way I always do, I hope, by making the best use of my time and generally attempting to fit a quart into a pint pot.' She gave a wry smile. 'Anyway, I don't have the luxury of living on independent means.' Her glance flicked over him. His suit was perfectly cut, beautifully tailored, and she doubted he had to worry too much about finances.

'True.' He sent her a sideways, curious look. 'But going on that way is bound to put a damper on your private life.'

She laughed. 'Well, there is that…but I don't actually have much of a private life right now.'

He frowned. 'Are you saying there's no boyfriend?'

'That's right.'

He let out a slow breath. 'I can't imagine what's wrong with the males around here,' he said, shaking his head.

'Nothing at all, I should think.' She sobered. 'I'm not overly concerned with getting involved right now. I had a bad experience with someone I thought I cared for, and who said he cared for me…it all went wrong, and I'm not keen to go there again any time soon. Anyway, there's too much going on for me now, with my studies and work, and so on.'

The break-up with Ewan had left scars, not ones that could be seen but her faith in human nature had been severely challenged. Perhaps she should have been fore-warned by her parents' example—they'd shown her that relationships could go badly wrong.

'I'm sorry. Do you want to talk about it?'

'No, not really.' She shrugged off all those troubling thoughts. 'The only thing that really matters is that I want to be a doctor, and if it means working hard to achieve that, that's what I'll do.'

'That's a splendid ambition.' He gave her an approv-ing look. 'Have you decided on a specialty yet? You seemed to be very much taken with the baby on the ward today.'

'Not yet, though I think I'm going to like working with children, even though it can be upsetting seeing them when they're ill. I was quite worried about baby George. I looked up his type of illness on the computer after ward rounds, and apparently most children with his problem grow out of it by the time they're two years old. It's so unfortunate that he has to be booked in for surgery.'

'Maybe. But he's been suffering from episodes of sleep apnoea, where he's been blue in the face through lack of oxygen, and that's far too dangerous to be ig-nored.'

'I know. The consultant explained, but it must still be hard for the parents to come to terms with it.'

They were getting closer to where she lived now, and she waved a hand towards a patch of green in the landscape, a small park bordered by black wrought-iron gates and fencing, an oasis in the midst of a built-up area. There were trees and shrubs in abundance, and through the railings she caught a glimpse of yellow daffodils swaying gently in the breeze, along with outcrops of tulips in all hues of scarlet through to the palest pink. The azaleas were in flower, too, glorious, exuberant blooms of deep crimson.

'I go there whenever I get the chance,' she said softly. 'I love the peace and quiet, and the colour all around me.'

He nodded. 'I like to go and stand by the Thames when I want to find peace. It's very calming to look out over the water, I find.' He looked around. 'Do you live close to here?'

'Yes. We're about half a mile from the Thames, I think. We're very lucky. The house is in a lovely, leafy terrace. It's very quiet, and I'm really happy to be living there.'

'We?' He raised a dark brow.

'My friends and I. We share. There's Matt and Lucy. Matt Berenger—I believe you know him.' He nodded acknowledgement, and Jade went on, 'Lucy's father actually owns the house, and he turned it over to students for these last few years. Matt's father's a business partner of Mr Clements, Lucy's father, and he arranged for him to have a place with us. As for me, Lucy and I have been friends for ever.'

'It sounds like a good arrangement.'

'It is.'

They turned into a tree-lined crescent, where a Georgian terrace of houses stood resplendent, touched by the dying rays of the sun. The buildings were three storeys high, white fronted, with wrought-iron railings at the windows and again at ground level. There was a small patch of lawn between the street railings and the houses were hung with baskets filled with spring flowers and trailing ivy.

'This is ours,' she said, stopping outside a house half-way along the terrace. 'We actually have a small garden out back. Talk about landing on my feet! I'm just so pleased to be living here.'

'I'm impressed,' Ben said, studying the building. 'If the inside's anything like the outside, you've every reason to be happy.'

She nodded. 'Come in with me, and I'll make you a coffee. It's the least I can do after the way you looked after me.'

'Are you sure?'

'Of course.' She could hardly let him go on his way after he'd taken the trouble to walk her home.

'Then I will, thanks.' His mouth curved, and she tried to ignore the warm glow that started up inside her. She didn't want to be enticed by his gentle manner and easygoing ways. She'd been there before with Ewan and the result hadn't been pleasant.

They walked up the few steps to the front door, and she showed him into the entrance hall. 'The lounge is through here,' she said, pushing open a door and leading the way into a large, high-ceilinged room with a polished wooden floor and deep sash windows. 'The furniture's a bit sparse, but at least it's comfortable. We do argue a bit over who gets to sit where, because even though there are two sofas, Matt and I both like to stretch out our legs when we get the chance. It does tend to make Lucy a bit annoyed at times.'

He chuckled. 'There are bound to be a few dis-agreements when several students live under one roof. Though three's probably a nice, manageable number.'

'True. But actually there used to be four of us until recently. Caroline left to take an elective course of study in Africa.' She sent him a quick glance. 'Which reminds me—I meant to ask if you did something else before taking up medicine. I have the feeling you might be two or three years older than Matt, who's in the same year as you—or perhaps I'm mistaken?'

He shook his head. 'You have it right. I took some time out to travel and see the world before I decided what I wanted to do. My parents were happy enough for me to do that, and I found temporary work wherever I could to support myself through it. Then, when I came back to the UK, I worked for a while in a hospital, on the administrative side. I just wanted to get a feel for things, to see if I'd be suited to the life.'

'And you obviously decided to go with it in the end. So medicine wins!' She grinned at him, and they did a high-five, their hands meeting in a spontaneous action that came out of nowhere. Ben was still smiling, gaz-ing around, when Lucy entered the room a second or two later, looking a bit frazzled.

Even frazzled, Lucy was stunning to look at, there was no doubt about it. With flowing golden hair and intensely blue eyes, she was a picture to behold. Her bone structure was perfect, her lips full and red, and her figure was absolutely perfect.

Jade glanced at Ben, curious to see what his reaction would be to her best friend. Most men did a double take and almost fell over themselves trying to get to know her.

Ben simply waited patiently to be introduced.

'Hello,' Lucy said, suddenly cottoning on to the fact that Jade wasn't alone. 'I don't think we've met, have we?'

'This is Ben,' Jade said. 'He's a friend of Matt's, a foundation-year doctor on placement with me. We met up today, and I was just going to offer him coffee.'

'Good idea.' Lucy held out her hand to him. 'It's great to meet you, Ben. I'm afraid Matt isn't here right now. He's gone to the all-night store to see if he can grab some pasties for supper.' She winced, and even that didn't mar her beauty. 'I forgot to get any food in, but...' she turned to look at Jade '...I'll do a full shop tomorrow, I promise.'

'That's okay. I managed to get something to eat at the café.' Jade frowned. 'I suppose you're still struggling with the cardiology project your consultant gave you?'

'Oh, that wretched thing! Tell me about it! I could almost wish Mr Sheldon hadn't decided I was to be his protégée. It's almost more work than I can handle. Along with the fact that I'm still trying to find someone to fill Caroline's boots.'

'The girl who left?' From his expression, it was clear

Ben's interest had been tweaked. 'Are you looking for someone else to move in here?'

Lucy nodded. 'That's right. I have to try and keep the rooms fully occupied. It's my father's house and he likes to keep things on a business footing.'

Ben smiled. 'Would I do as a tenant? It just so happens that I'm looking to move. I've been renting a place across the river for the last six months, but the lease is up, and now that I'm based at the hospital over here, I'd rather be close by.'

'Oh…really? Well, I'm certainly looking for someone, and you *are* a friend of Matt's after all…' Lucy was thinking, talking to herself, but Jade could see that she was taken with the idea. 'You'd need to supply references.'

'That's not a problem.'

Lucy brightened, and it was as if the sun had come out. 'Perhaps I should show you around?' she suggested, heading towards the door. 'Each room's pretty much self-contained, with a toilet and wash-basin, and there are a couple of bathrooms, which we have to share. You'll also find that there's a table and chair in your room so that you'll be able to study in peace whenever you like.'

'That sounds like just what I'm looking for.' Ben half turned and glanced at Jade, and she guessed he was uncomfortable at following Lucy out of the room and leaving her alone.

'It's okay, you go ahead,' Jade murmured. 'I'll make the coffee.'

'If you're sure?'

'I am.'

She gazed at the door for a while after they had gone. She frowned. It was disturbing to think that he might very soon be coming here to live with them. It wasn't at all what she had expected, and somehow it troubled her. It was one thing to be working alongside him, but having him stay here in such close proximity was quite another. The very idea had knocked her off balance, and now all of her defences were suddenly on standby.

CHAPTER TWO

'HE'S not bad at all, is he?' Lucy dropped hot crumpets onto a plate and began to toast another batch.

'Um—who's this we're talking about?' Jade dragged her attention away from the magazine she was reading, and was rewarded with a sharp hiss of breath and a shake of the head.

'Ben, of course. Our soon-to-be housemate.' Lucy frowned at her. 'You haven't been listening to a word I've said, have you?'

'I have…' Jade pulled herself up with a guilty start. 'You were talking about him moving in here.' She tried to recall what Lucy had said. 'He won't be making the move straight away because he has a few loose ends to tie up…and he needs a day or two to pack up his bits and pieces, especially his new leather reclining chair that he absolutely won't do without and a desk with drawers that are crammed full of his paperwork.' Her brows knitted together. Obviously, he wasn't a great believer in saving the trees.

'That was ten minutes ago,' Lucy said crossly. 'I've moved on since then.' She jabbed a finger at the plate. 'And these crumpets are meant to be eaten while they're hot.' She looked over Jade's shoulder at the magazine. 'What's that you're reading, anyway? It seems to be keeping you pretty well absorbed.'

'It's the student paper.' Jade put the magazine to one side and started to butter crumpets. She passed a couple of them to Matt, who was sitting across the other side of the table, checking web pages.

'Thanks,' he said. 'I didn't know the new edition had come out yet.'

She smiled. 'I got it hot off the press from a friend who works in the print room. Guess who's editing the mag now that the union rep has stepped down?'

'Who?'

'Your friend, Ben.'

She passed the magazine to him. 'He's introduced a new cartoon feature in there—it has his signature on it, so I guess he designed it himself. He's called the series *Med-life Crises*—I'm sure it's based on the goings on of some of the fifth-year medical students. This month's storyline is very like something that happened in lectures a few weeks ago...only he's made it seem much funnier somehow.'

Matt turned the page, and Lucy abandoned the crumpets to lean over and read the cartoon with him. She began to laugh. 'Oh, that's clever. I like that!' She shot a glance at Jade. 'He has a wicked sense of humour. I remember those lectures.'

'The tutors roped in volunteers from around the medical school,' Jade explained to Matt, 'and were trying to teach us about patient-doctor communication skills through role playing. One of the students told her patient he needed to go on a fitness regime and lose some weight. He wasn't too pleased, and she found out later that he's her new consultant.' She was still chuckling. 'I wouldn't have dared print that, just in case either of them saw it and took offence.'

'It doesn't seem as if Ben has any qualms about that.' Matt bit into a crumpet, licking the melted butter off his lips.

'No. As I was saying…' Lucy looked pointedly at Jade '… I think he'll fit in here really well. He seems to be quite easygoing and keen to get on with his studies. None of this clattering about of an evening with guitars and fiddling about with amplifiers.' She sent Matt an accusing stare.

He lifted his shoulders and raised his flattened palms in a dismissive gesture. 'So I practise my music occasionally—it's not as though I'm working on it till all hours, every day of the week.'

'Just as well, or one of these days you might get ready to rock and find your amplifier has been disconnected.'

They scowled at one another, and Jade sighed. She bit into a crumpet. It was hard to imagine Ben sitting with them at the breakfast table. Truth to tell, she was still having trouble coming to terms with the fact that he was actually going to be living there. It didn't sit right with her somehow, and she couldn't quite work out what was wrong.

Maybe it was a vague feeling that he was out of her league. He and his friends all seemed so much more confident than she was, and perhaps that was because their backgrounds were very different from hers in the main. Her family had always worked and struggled to get by, whereas Ben's parents were in business and were comparatively rich, by all accounts. From what Matt had told her, the business was doing extremely well, with offshoots in Europe and Scandinavia.

There was no point dwelling on any of it, though. It was going to happen whether she wanted it or not.

She wiped her fingers on a paper towel and looked at Matt. 'Are you back in A and E this morning?'

He nodded. 'In the trauma unit to begin with, and then I'll be working in the fracture clinic this afternoon.' He glanced at his watch. 'In fact, I'd better head off now. I'm due at a meeting to go over the details of yesterday's cases.'

'Me, too. I'm supposed to be at the hospital for eight o'clock.'

Matt left the house, and Jade set about clearing the table, carefully stacking the dishes in the sink and filling the washing-up bowl with hot, soapy water. She glanced at Lucy. 'I get the feeling you're looking forward to having Ben here with us. He must have made quite an impression on you.' Lucy didn't normally react with any great enthusiasm to newcomers—at least, not the male variety. She was too used to fending them off, though perhaps she'd made an exception in Ben's case.

'Yeah, he's all right.' Lucy grinned. 'It turned out to be a lucky move all round, you bringing him home with you the other day.'

'Hmm. Maybe.'

Perhaps there was something in the way she said it that caught Lucy's attention, because her expression sobered. 'Do you have some misgivings?' She threw Jade a cautious glance. 'It's just that it seemed like a heaven-sent opportunity after Caroline's room was left empty.'

Jade smiled. 'I'm sure things will work out just fine. It all happened so quickly. I only asked him in because he'd helped me and he was thoughtful enough to walk me home afterwards, and the next thing he's going to be living with us. It takes a bit of getting used to.'

They finished tidying the kitchen and set off to walk to the hospital. The sky was a cloudless blue, and the City looked fresh and sparkling in the morning sunshine. Jade made up her mind to put all her doubts behind her and instead give her concentration to the work ahead. In the weeks coming up to her final exams, things were going to be pretty hectic and she needed to be on the ball the whole time.

'Good luck in Cardiology,' she told Lucy as they parted company. Lucy was having a difficult time in her placement, and if yesterday was anything to go by Jade couldn't expect to fare much better. It looked as though her consultant was given to asking searching questions whenever they met up for patient reviews or ward rounds, and it seemed she would have to get used to thinking on her feet.

The first hour or so of the morning was spent in going over the case notes of patients who had been admitted to the paediatric ward the previous day, followed by a visit to the neonatal unit.

'How are we going to assess this child?' Professor Farnham wanted to know as they stopped by a cot. He was in his fifties, tall and dark haired, slimly built, a man whose whole body and manner hinted at ceaseless energy and a thirst for knowledge. 'What are we looking for?'

Jade drew in a deep breath and checked the baby's file. The baby was only three days old, a tiny, preterm infant who whimpered softly in his crib. His arms flailed weakly and his mouth quivered as he gave a helpless cry. More than anything, she wanted to pick him up and hold him to her, to feel his warm, soft body in her arms.

Instead, she tried to dredge up all she had learned about neonatal problems. 'The history shows that he has had several seizures,' she said. 'He's been vomiting and he isn't feeding well, according to his mother.' The mother wasn't around to hear their discussion, thankfully. The nurse had taken her into the office so that she could talk to her about any worries that might be weighing her down.

'The first course of action would be to take blood tests and check serum chemistries. I'm thinking there might be a problem with the levels of calcium or magnesium in the blood. Then I would do urine tests in case of any renal problems. We should get an ECG as well, to check for any cardiac rhythm abnormalities.' She hesitated momentarily. 'The mother has a history of diabetes, so it's possible there might be some connection between that and the baby's problems.'

'Good thinking.' The professor beamed. 'I'll leave you in charge of all that. Depending on the results of the tests, we might need to do some X-rays later. Let me know when the reports come back from the lab.'

'I will.'

He swept out of the room a minute or so later, and Jade let out a long, slow breath. Was this just a foretaste of her upcoming clinical examination finals? She was going to be a junior doctor soon, so she needed to have these skills at her fingertips.

At least Ben hadn't been around to witness her being put on the spot once again. Paediatrics was a new specialty for her, and she'd had to do a lot of research over the last few weeks to give her an idea of the kind of things she might be dealing with. Even so, she was a bit worried about putting on a good show.

She gently stroked the baby's silky hair, and then lightly traced a line over the velvet-soft skin of his tiny hand. He gripped her finger, clinging on to her, his eyes widening and his mouth puckering in eager anticipation. She chuckled, enjoying the moment.

'You're a little sweetheart, aren't you?' she murmured. 'I wish I didn't have to put you through all these tests, but I have to find out what's wrong with you so that we can put it right. I'll be really gentle, I promise.' She gazed at him for a moment or two longer and then carefully withdrew her finger from his grasp. 'I have to go and find a syringe, and some vials, and some forms for the lab. I'll be back in a minute.'

When she returned a short while later, she was startled to find Ben standing by the cot. He looked good. He was smartly dressed in dark trousers and a crisp linen shirt with the cuffs rolled back, showing forearms made golden by the sun. His tie was a silk blend, in a subtle blue-grey design that complemented the pale blue of his shirt. He looked every bit the doctor who was in full control of everything around him.

He had set up a monitor to record the baby's heart rate—it was slow, she noticed. He was checking the baby's case file, and every now and again he glanced at the infant and his eyes crinkled in a faint smile. He looked up as Jade approached.

'Hello, there,' he said, his gaze moving over her appreciatively. 'I was hoping we would meet up again fairly soon. I know it's likely to be a bit hit and miss, because you have lectures and study periods every so often.'

'That's right,' she acknowledged, 'but not today. Professor Farnham has asked me to do a work-up on young Sammy.'

He nodded. 'Yes, the professor told me.' He looked at the baby and frowned. 'According to the records, Sammy's having fairly frequent seizures, some heart rhythm abnormalities, and his blood pressure is low. Not a good start in life, is it?'

She shook her head. 'I must confess I'm a bit over-awed working with newborns. Perhaps you've put your finger on the problem. It's the emotional factor—it seems so unfair that they're burdened with illness from the moment they arrive in the world.'

He laid a hand on her shoulder in a gesture of support. 'I'm sure you'll get used to it, given time. You're here to help them through it…try looking at it that way.'

'I will.'

He glanced at the trolley she had prepared. 'I see you're set up to take blood samples. Are you okay with that?'

She pulled a face. 'I don't usually have a problem taking blood from adults, or even from older children, like teenagers, but babies are different, aren't they? They look so fragile, and they don't know what's happening to them, and I suppose it's a bit daunting.'

'Would you like me to hold him and distract him while you do the business?'

A feeling of relief ran through her. 'Would you mind? That would be really good.'

'Not at all.' He lifted the baby from the cot and held him carefully in the crook of his arm. He seemed perfectly at ease with his precious bundle, and Jade watched him, unexpectedly sidetracked for a while by the tenderness of the moment.

'Now, then, young Sammy,' Ben murmured, 'what can we do to keep your mind off things?' He was thoughtful for a second or two, and then he reached into his trousers pocket and drew out his keys. 'Here we are. Just the thing.'

He looked at Jade, and said quietly, 'All set?'

She nodded, and Ben jangled his keys to distract the baby while she took the blood sample. It was all over in a matter of seconds.

Relieved, she labelled the vials and smiled at Ben. 'Well, I have to say it would be great to have you around every time I have to do that.'

'I'll see what I can do about it,' he said, laughing. He placed the baby back in the cot and took a moment to settle him, before turning to watch as she began to write out the lab forms. Her ponytail fell softly against her cheek, and she brushed it back out of the way.

'I like your hair,' he observed softly. 'It's beautiful, like silk.'

She gave him a startled look, pausing as she sealed the vial in its plastic pocket. 'Thank you. The truth is, I like my sleep too much and so I didn't have time to do more than just tie it back this morning.' She dropped the needle into the sharps bin and began to tidy up the equipment she had used.

'At the café bar you had it pinned up, I recall.' His smoky, grey-blue eyes glimmered as his glance moved over her. 'Either way, you're a knockout. I somehow get the feeling you're not going to be too good for my blood pressure whenever we're around one another.'

She had a vague suspicion that could work both ways. 'Well, I'm sorry about that,' she murmured, 'but I'm sure you'll manage somehow.' She liked him, but she wasn't going to respond to his flirting. She couldn't. Her time with Ewan had taught her that flirtation could get out of hand, and lead to some heavy involvement, and before you knew it you were embroiled in a situation that was bounding out of control. She couldn't go through that again. It had been over months ago but she was still raw and hurting.

She gave him a sympathetic glance. 'Some people say a cold shower does the trick.'

He gave a rueful laugh. 'You're not going to take pity on me, are you? I had in mind a much more romantic prescription.'

She smiled. 'Yes, I'm sure you did, but I think I prefer to keep my mind on the job.'

He looked at her thoughtfully. 'Whoever he was, this man who upset you and caused you to put up your defences has a lot to answer for. I think you should know that we're not all the same.'

'Maybe.' She straightened up, getting ready to push the trolley back into the office. 'But I'd just as soon not put it to the test.' She frowned. 'So I'm going to take these samples along to the lab. Are you going to be in the neonatal unit for a while?' With any luck, he'd say no, and she would be able to get on with her work without feeling hot and bothered because he was close by.

He followed her to the door. 'Yes, I have to keep an eye on young Sammy. Professor Farnham suggested that I leave you to do the procedures and think through the results, but I have to take day-to-day responsibility for him and report back to the professor.'

'Oh, I see.' So much for her hopes. 'Well, I suppose I'm glad I'm not being thrown in at the deep end. I know I'll have to do this kind of thing on my own all the while when I'm a foundation-year doctor, but just at the moment I'm sort of feeling my way.'

'It'll get easier. The first few months as a junior doctor can be hard on the nerves, but after that you kind of get the hang of things.' He opened the door for her. 'How about you and I meet up and have lunch down by the river later on? You can fill me in on the set up back at the house—who does what, whether there are any rotas for getting in the groceries and cleaning, and so on.'

She frowned. 'Won't you be on call? I mean, what if you're paged?'

'That's okay. The registrar will be on duty to provide cover and, anyway, it won't take long to get back here if need be. That's the beauty of working in this place, we're very close to the Thames.'

'I suppose so.' She frowned. 'As to lunch, I'm not sure... I was planning on going to the library to study. Perhaps some other time.' She would be seeing a lot of him over the next few months, she knew she had to get used to that idea, but even so, her instincts were warning her that if it was at all possible, she ought to keep some distance between them.

He forestalled her when she would have left the room, placing a hand on her arm. 'You need to take a break—a proper break. It's good to relax—it helps to clear your mind and revitalise you. That way you'll be able to do your job so much better.'

She chuckled, admiring his persistence. 'Really? Is that what you do? Now I see why you're so fond of your reclining chair. Lucy said you couldn't do without it.'

'It's true.' He feigned a serious expression. 'I do some of my best thinking in that chair.'

She shook her head. 'Maybe you can get by on a quick read through of information, but I'm afraid I can't. Unfortunately, I have to knuckle down and study hard.'

'All the more reason to take a proper lunch hour. I'll come and find you around one o'clock.' He waved a hand and disappeared back inside the unit.

Her mouth dropped open a fraction as she watched him go. He didn't mean to give up, did he?

She took the blood samples and forms over to the lab, and spent a few minutes chatting to the pathologist. She got on well with him, and knew that he would get back to her with his report as soon as he was able.

When she walked back into the neonatal unit a little later, she was relieved to find that the coast was clear. Ben was nowhere to be seen.

'He was called to Paediatrics,' Alice, the nurse on duty, told her. She pulled a mournful face. 'Such a shame. I could so get used to working with him.'

Jade smiled, and Alice chuckled, her silky black hair shifting and settling as she moved her head. 'He's good-natured, too,' she said. 'I can see he'll be great on the children's ward.'

'He is,' Jade agreed. 'I was with him in Paediatrics a few days back, and the youngsters loved him. I wonder if he's found his vocation?'

'Oh, surely not? That has to be here, with me, I'm certain of it.' Alice grinned and pulled a trolley from a side room. 'For the urine testing,' she explained, indicating the equipment that was set out on sterile cloths. 'You said that was your next job.'

'So I did. Thanks, Alice. I'll get to it.'

Jade was busy for the next hour or so, checking up on Sammy and the other babies in the unit. She even managed to sit with one three-week-old infant, nestling her in her arms while the baby sucked at a bottle of milk formula, making small gasping and gurgling noises. Her delicate complexion was peaches and cream, with a smattering of milk-rash spots across her nose and cheeks.

'You're beautiful,' Jade murmured, watching as the baby sucked hungrily. 'I think I want one just like you.' Her expression was wistful.

The time flew by, and she was deeply immersed in her work when Ben came back into the unit. 'Are you ready to go?' he queried. 'Can I help you finish what you're doing?'

'Is it that time already?' she murmured, glancing up at him. She finished examining the infant she was with, and folded her stethoscope into her pocket. Maybe her library study could wait. It would be good to get out in the fresh air. 'I just have to make a note of the prescription medicines, and I'll be with you.'

Ben checked the oxygen flow being delivered to the baby in the specialised cot, and then he bent over and lightly stroked the infant's leg. 'She still has her legs curled as though she's in the womb,' he said softly. 'They're so tiny, these premature babies, aren't they? They're barely much bigger than my hand.'

She nodded. It brought a lump to her throat to see such a strong man being so gentle with a helpless infant. 'There,' she said after a while, 'I'm all finished. I'm ready to leave now.'

'Good. We'll stop to pick up some lunch to go from the cafeteria, on the way.'

'All right.'

The air was fresh and sweet as they left the hospital and walked along the streets towards the river. They found a bench seat along the walkway where they could sit and eat, and spend time looking out over the glittering water. Jade watched the leisure boats drifting by, and listened to the birds calling overhead.

'I hope they're not after our lunch,' she said, her mouth making a wry curve. 'I've heard that gulls have been known to swoop down and take the food from people's hands.'

'Nah. They're a better class of bird around here.' He looked in the paper bag he was holding. 'I'm sure they're not partial to sausage rolls and Chelsea buns... a brown trout instead, maybe, or a tasty chub.'

'That's just as well, because I am. There's something about sausage pasties that really gets my taste buds flowing.' She flipped the lid on her coffee carton. 'Mmm... this is good,' she said, swallowing the hot liquid. 'Just what I needed.'

He handed her a sausage roll wrapped in a serviette and she bit into it hungrily. 'This is great,' she said, savouring the taste. 'It's still warm from the oven, the way I like it.' She laughed. 'At least I get to eat it all to myself. If my brother's around, and there are sausage rolls or pasties anywhere in the house, no one gets a look in.'

He smiled at her enjoyment of the food. 'Do you have just the one brother?'

'Actually, I have three altogether, and Ross, the one who likes pasties, is the youngest. The others are older than me.'

'That sounds like quite a houseful.'

She nodded. 'What about you? Do you have any brothers?'

'A sister. She's younger than me and works with my

father in the business—it's a packaging company. Sarah runs the office down in Hampshire.'

'Is that where your family live—in Hampshire?'

'That's right. We have a rambling old house in a beautiful village down there. We're close to the forest, and not too far from the sea.'

His expression was remote for a second or two, and she said quietly, 'It sounds as though you wish you were back there.'

His mouth curved. 'Yes, I think I do. It's where I was born and brought up.'

'Didn't you think of doing your training back there?'

'I did, but the programme that was offered here in London tempted me more. I suppose my parents instilled in me the need to be focussed, to achieve my full potential, and that's what I'm trying to do.'

He was thoughtful for a while. 'I have my sights set on specialising in paediatrics, possibly in paediatric A and E. It's important to me that I get the very best experiences possible, so for the next year or so I'll be working really hard at all my assessments. I want my e-portfolio to be filled with top-grade achievements. I don't want to simply get by in medicine. I want to be at the top of my field.'

'That's a huge challenge.'

'Yes, it is. And in the end, when the time's right, I can always go back home to Hampshire.'

'There is that.' He was ambitious, that was for sure.

She studied him from under her lashes, amusement in her green eyes as a thought occurred to her. 'So, with all that work, I imagine there'll be no time for any serious romantic entanglements where you're concerned, will there? All these nurses that are pining for you back at the hospital are going to be seriously disappointed, aren't they?'

'Are they really pining for me?' He looked surprised, then shook his head. 'Oh, I don't know about that.' He dipped into the paper bag and brought out a fruit bun. His expression was mischievous. 'Still, a little bit of flirting here and there never hurt anyone, did it...especially with the right person. After all, life's for living, don't you think?' He dangled the bun in front of her, tantalising her with the sweet, fruity aroma. 'Can I tempt you?'

Her green eyes sparked with amusement. 'If it's buns we're talking, oh, yes, please, definitely.' She breathed in the scent of cinnamon spice, and her mouth began to water in anticipation. But then she realised she might be treading on dangerous ground, and she said softly, 'Anything else, though, and you can forget it, I'm afraid. I'm not in the market.'

No way. Not even a tiny bit would she give in to any silly ideas that her wildly overactive hormones might be suggesting. A little flirting here and there? Not on your life. Not with him, at any rate...the stakes were far too high.

He passed the bun to her and gave a wry smile. 'That's a very definitive statement,' he said slowly. 'I'll have to see if I can change your mind on that one.'

CHAPTER THREE

JADE found herself thinking about that lunchtime meeting a couple of days later. In spite of her reservations about getting to know Ben better, she had to admit she enjoyed being with him. He had such a tolerant, friendly manner and a gentle sense of humour. It was no surprise that everybody liked him.

She could see him now, out of the corner of her eye, flawlessly clad in dark trousers, freshly laundered shirt and tie, leaning negligently against the nurses' station, chatting with Mandy, the nurse in charge of the ward. They looked relaxed and comfortable, and all at once Jade felt a twinge of regret that she couldn't share that same easy relationship with him. Instead, whenever she was around him lately, it seemed her alarm system went into overdrive. She was way too conscious of him as a virile, energetic male, and she was beginning to realise that it would be all too easy for her to go along with his teasing invitations.

She took a deep breath and brought her attention back to the case notes she was supposed to be studying. A child had been referred to hospital by his GP and

Professor Farnham wanted her to work with Ben on this case. He wanted her to take the lead.

'You look worried,' Ben said, appearing by her side, out of the blue. 'Is there a problem? Are you bothered about doing the work-up on the seven-year-old who was brought in this morning?'

'Um… I'm okay, thanks.' It was a lie. How could she be all right when he was so close to her that she could feel the warmth coming from him, when his long, muscular body was almost touching hers? She didn't want to be affected by him in any way, but in spite of herself she could feel her blood beginning to heat.

She cleared her throat and dragged her attention back to the task in hand. 'We're both going to be looking after the boy, aren't we?' she said. 'I'm all right with that. If I seem worried it's just that my mind's all over the place at the moment. With the combination of work at the hospital, the café bar and studying for exams, I'm in a bit of a spin. Right now, my head's back in neonatal with the babies.' She hadn't even mentioned the strain of having her every move monitored. Professor Farnham was very thorough in everything he did, and it was only to be expected. After all, lives were at stake.

Ben was frowning and she guessed she probably wasn't making much sense to him, so she added, 'I was over there this morning, checking on Sammy.'

'The baby who was having seizures?'

'That's right.' She smiled. 'He's doing much better since we managed to identify the cause of his illness and start the treatment.' She made a vague gesture with her hands. 'Well, you know all about him, of course,

since he's your patient. I'm really pleased that the medication is working so well. I suppose I hadn't expected
it to happen so quickly.'

'It's not unusual, apparently. A good many newborns
are affected by hypocalcaemia, especially if their mothers are diabetic. The mothers become low in magnesium, which means that their babies are affected, too.'

She nodded. 'The professor was quizzing me on it.'
Recalling the moment, she put a hand to her chest in
a mixture of anxiety and relief. 'Luckily, I'd read up
on it. It causes a problem with the babies' parathyroid
glands and they end up not having enough calcium in
their blood.'

'Yes. I suppose a lot of things could be traced back
to the mother's health and diet.' His gaze followed the
movement of her hand, and she was immediately conscious of the up-and-down motion of her chest. The
soft cotton fabric of her top clung to her breasts and
made her uneasily aware of her gently curving feminine shape. Flustered, she let her hand fall to her side.

He hesitated for a moment or two, as though struggling to keep his mind on track, but then he pulled
himself together and said, 'It's, uh…easily treated with
intravenous calcium gluconate. Eventually things sort
themselves out and the babies start to function normally…which is just as well, because Sammy sort of
pulls at your heart, doesn't he, being so tiny?'

'Yes, he does.' She glanced at him. He seemed distracted. Was he as conscious as she was of the sudden
tension that had sprung up between them?

His glance drifted over her, gliding along the swell

of her hip outlined by the gently flowing skirt she was wearing, before returning to dwell on the pink flush of her cheeks. 'I…uh…' He made a visible effort to get back to the matter in hand. 'I thought you did really well to come up with the diagnosis.'

'Yes…well, I'm glad I can chalk that one up as a success.' How on earth was she going to cope when he came to live at the house? Then there would be nowhere to hide, no means of escape.

At least she had one more day of ultimate freedom, because he'd said he wouldn't be moving in until the weekend. Apparently, it would be easier for him to transfer his belongings then, because a friend was loaning him the use of a large van.

'Are you sure you're okay? You seem to have drifted off somewhere.' His deep voice cut into her thoughts and she came back to reality with a bump. He looked concerned.

'I'm fine,' she said. 'I'm just hoping we'll have the same success with the seven-year-old and his rash.'

'Hmm.' She could see he was mulling things over. 'I know I've said this before, but isn't there any way you could cut down on your hours at the café?'

She shook her head, bracing herself for action and already on the move. 'No. And anyway it isn't necessary. You can relax. I'm on top of things.'

He went with her to the side ward where the little boy was lying in bed, clearly ill looking and hooked up to monitors, while his anxious mother sat in a chair at the bedside.

Jade aimed a surreptitious look in Ben's direction.

Where his patients were concerned, he always had that look of someone who was totally in control of the situation, comfortably sure of himself and giving the overall impression that he could be relied on to put things right. He was a junior doctor, still under probation himself, so to speak, and yet he always commanded respect. From what she'd seen, Professor Farnham obviously had lots of faith in him.

She braced herself. One way or another, she had to prove she was equally worthy.

'Hello, Mrs Granger…hello, Owen,' she greeted them, in a friendly fashion. 'I'm Jade Blythe, a fifth-year medical student, and this is Dr Langley. We're here to take a look at Owen, and to talk to you about any worries you might have. I understand you were referred here this morning by your GP?'

'Yes, that's right. It's this rash, you see,' the woman said quickly. 'As soon as I saw it, I rushed him to the doctor. He's not been well for a while—he had a chest infection just a couple of weeks ago, and now this. And he's in such a lot of pain—so much that he can't walk. The nurse had to find a wheelchair to bring him here.' She kept her voice low, aware of her son, poorly but alert, taking everything in.

'I understand.' Jade smiled at Owen. 'Is it all right if I examine you?' she asked.

He nodded. 'My knees hurt,' he said. 'And my tummy.' He clutched his hand to his abdomen, and then looked at his mother, his mouth quivering. 'I want my dad to be here as well. Is he coming?'

'Yes, he'll come as soon as he can.' His mother's eyes

were shadowed, her voice thin, and Jade wondered what was wrong that made her look away.

Owen subsided against the pillows. He looked pale and tired, his face peaky, all the more noticeable because of the shock of tousled brown hair that framed his features. Jade wanted to comfort him and tell him that all would be well, but she couldn't easily do that, not at this stage, when it was clear that something was definitely wrong.

'I see you have the rash over your legs and bottom,' she said, in a while. The rest of his body had escaped relatively unscathed, but where the rash existed it was reddish purple in colour, and she was immediately worried.

Ben picked up a drinking glass and pressed it against a purple patch on the boy's leg. 'There's no blanching,' he murmured. 'It doesn't disappear when you press it.'

'No.' Jade quickly ran through in her mind all she knew about rashes. Everyone feared meningitis, but this child's symptoms specifically involved joint and abdominal pain, and she was pretty sure it was due to something else. Anyway, Professor Farnham was already giving the boy antibiotic cover, in case of any lingering infection from his earlier chest complaint.

She fastened a blood-pressure cuff around the boy's arm and explained to him what she was doing. 'This is a clever little machine,' she told him. 'It measures the blood flow inside your body and then gives us some numbers so that we can see how you're doing.'

The readings added to her concerns. His blood pressure was raised and when she took his temperature she found that he had a low-grade fever.

'I don't feel very well,' the boy said, his mouth down-turned, his expression thoroughly miserable.

Ben moved forward and laid a reassuring hand on his arm. 'Why don't you lie back and rest?' he suggested in a soothing voice. 'I'm sure you'll be feeling better in a while. The doctor who saw you a little while ago gave you some medicine, didn't he? That should start to work very soon—it should take away the pain and lower your temperature.'

Jade glanced at Ben. 'We should run blood tests to see if there's any infection present, and get urine samples to monitor his kidney function. I'd suggest keeping an eye on fluid and electrolyte balance, too. Do you think we ought to prescribe an antihypertensive to bring his blood pressure down?'

'I'm in complete agreement with you about all the tests—let's get them started right away. As to blood-pressure medication, it's definitely an option, but his blood pressure isn't dangerously high, so I think we should wait and see what the lab results are first. We don't want to start it and then find it interferes with any other medication we might need to prescribe.'

'Okay. I'll get on and organise things.'

A short time later, when she had finished obtaining samples and writing up the laboratory forms, she stopped for a moment to study the child. He was restless and uncomfortable, but his eyelids were drooping and an occasional yawn escaped him. 'How about if I get the play leader to find a video for you to watch?'

she said quietly. 'You can tell her which ones you like.'
If they could divert his attention in some way, he would
probably soon fall asleep.

'Yes, please, I'd like that.'

Jade moved away from the bedside and paged the
play leader, and then gave the samples and forms to a
nurse so that they could be taken over to the lab for urgent analysis.

Ben smiled at her. 'That was a good idea, involving
the play leader,' he said under his breath.

'I thought it might take his mind off things,' she
murmured. 'Besides, I've a feeling something's troubling his mother. It might give me the chance to draw
her away for a few minutes, so that I can talk to her.'

He nodded, looking at her with renewed respect.
'Women's intuition?' His expression was regretful. 'I
sometimes wish I could be that perceptive.'

A short time later, when Owen was engrossed in
watching a video, Jade led his mother away from the
bedside. 'Perhaps we could go somewhere quiet and
have a chat,' she suggested. It might do her some good
to be given a sympathetic ear and to be able to unbur-
den herself.

Ben probably guessed that it would be more produc-
tive if the two women were left alone. 'I'll stay and keep
Owen company,' he said.

Jade nodded, turning to look at them fleetingly as
she left the room. They had their backs to her and their
dark heads were together, the man and the boy united
for that moment in time, chuckling as a cartoon cat fell

over his tail. 'He's going to fall down the hole,' Owen predicted, his voice rising in eager anticipation. 'He is.'

'Do you think so? Wait for it…wait for it… Yup, there he goes!' Ben laughed with him.

Jade's mouth curved, and she left them to it, leading the boy's mother along the corridor to the relatives' waiting room. There was a coffee machine in there, and she handed a cup of the reviving brew to the unhappy woman.

'It's actually quite good coffee, considering that it's from a machine,' she murmured, sitting down beside her on the upholstered bench.

'Thank you.' Mrs Granger managed a weak smile, and they talked for a while about her son and his illness.

'Everything depends on what the tests reveal, of course,' Jade said, 'but it's possible that Owen could be suffering from a condition that involves inflammation of the blood vessels. It's usually an autoimmune reaction to something, possibly to the infection he's had recently, but the disease is fairly self-limiting. The rash is really a kind of bruising. Treatment is generally supportive, and the condition quite often clears up on its own. Of course, we will make sure that Owen is comfortable and do everything possible to help him to get well.'

'So you don't think he has meningitis, or even a form of juvenile arthritis?'

'No, I don't but, as I said, we must wait for the test results.' She studied the woman briefly. 'Does Owen have any brothers or sisters?'

Mrs Granger nodded. 'He has two sisters. They both seem to be healthy enough. They're at school at the moment, so I don't have to worry too much about them while I'm here at the hospital with Owen. I'll have to make some arrangements for them to be looked after this evening and tomorrow, though.' She frowned, thinking about it. 'I expect my neighbour will help out. She's usually very good.'

Jade frowned. 'Don't you have a husband who can help out?'

She shook her head. 'He left us, a year ago...more than a year ago.' Her voice faltered. 'It's been difficult... for me and for the children. I'm not really used to handling things on my own. I'm getting there, I suppose, but it isn't easy.'

A small shiver of recognition ran along Jade's spine. 'I can imagine.' She knew something of what the woman was going through and compassion welled up inside her. 'It must be hard for you to cope with three young children to look after all by yourself. Does your husband know that Owen is ill?'

'Yes. I told him. I phoned him this morning after we'd been to see the doctor. He's at work, but he's going to come over here as soon as he can.'

'That's something, then. Does he see the children regularly?'

'It works out at about once a fortnight, I suppose.' Mrs Granger's expression was grim. 'It's very unsettling for them. They don't really understand what's going on.'

'I'm sorry.' Her words struck a chord with Jade. Her

own family had suffered similar problems. It was clear to see that the woman was distressed, and Jade wanted to help, but she didn't know how to go about it. She could barely skim the surface. 'Do you have any family who could be with you at this time? Your parents, or a brother or sister, maybe?'

'I hadn't thought about it. I was in such a panic when I had to bring Owen here. I haven't had time to think properly.' She looked at Jade, her hazel eyes clearing a little. 'Perhaps I could ring my sister—I'm sure she would want to come over.'

'That's a good idea. Why don't you do it now?' Jade suggested. 'And then, perhaps you'd like to come back to sit with Owen? You could get some food from the cafeteria, if you like. It might make you feel a bit better.'

'I'll do that. Thanks.'

Jade stood up. 'I'll leave you to it, then. I'll be back to look at Owen in a while, and I'll let you know about the tests as soon as I have the results. In the meantime, the nurse will be around to look after both of you.'

Jade guessed she would want some privacy to make the call, and went back to check on Owen. Thankfully, he was asleep, and Ben was switching off the video player.

'Is everything all right?' he asked, shooting her a glance.

She nodded. 'I think so.' Her expression was sombre as her mind went over everything Mrs Granger had confided in her. 'She's phoning her sister to see if she'll come and give her some support.'

'That's good. But I really meant, are you all right? You seem to be preoccupied. Is it just that you're concerned about Owen, or is there something else?'

Her eyes widened at his insight. 'I'm troubled, of course, because he's unwell, but it isn't that. It's just that...' she frowned '... while I was talking to Mrs Granger, she told me about her family circumstances. She's separated from her husband. They've been apart for more than a year, so I suppose it isn't likely that they'll be getting back together any time soon.'

He sent her a thoughtful look. 'It's a sad state of affairs, but stuff happens. It would be great if all marriages were made in heaven, but unfortunately life isn't like that.'

'No.' The word stuck in her throat, and she tried to ignore the surge in her emotions, busying herself by looking at Owen's chart. His temperature had dropped slightly.

'I can't help thinking there's something more—something you're not telling me.' Ben's deep voice intruded on her thoughts.

Perhaps he'd picked up on the defensive note in her quick answer. Nothing much escaped him, did it? She shrugged awkwardly. 'As you say, it's life. It isn't all blue skies and sunshine, is it? There's a lot of rain, too.'

'And you've experienced some of that? Is this to do with your family, or your ex? I'm just guessing here, but I can't help thinking it might help if you were to talk things through.'

A bleak smile crossed her mouth. 'I wish that were true, but some things can't be mended. Anyway, it was all a long time ago. There's no point in raking over old ground.'

He laid a hand on her arm, stopping her quick movements. 'Put the chart down and talk to me,' he said. 'Whatever it is, you don't have to keep it locked inside. You can trust me.'

She looked at him, her green eyes troubled. She wasn't convinced that talking about it would help, but she knew instinctively that she could put her faith in Ben. He wouldn't let anyone down—not when matters were serious.

She hooked the chart over the end of the bed. Would it hurt to share her thoughts with him?

She said softly, 'The thing is, I know how Mrs Granger must be feeling, because the same thing happened to my mother, years ago.'

'Your father left her?'

'Yes. She was distraught, and we didn't know what to do or say to comfort her—but, then, we were very young. I was ten when he walked out and my younger brother was only six. James and Tom were around twelve and seventeen. It was a bad time for all of us.' She sighed, remembering how it had been. 'We all tried to help her, but it was hard because we were suffering, too. If you lose a father, you think the world has come to an end.'

Her mouth flattened. 'It seemed as though he'd not given us a second thought, and in a way that felt worse than if he'd died. My brothers were anxious and upset, a bit rebellious for quite some time afterwards, because they didn't know how to handle the situation. For my-

self, I felt guilty, as though it was in some way my
fault. Had I done something to make him go away? He
couldn't have loved me if he'd taken off with barely a
word. Obviously, I meant nothing to him and he'd abandoned me.'

Ben's arm circled her shoulders, and she was aware
of instant warmth and comfort as he drew her to him.
He was inviting her to lean on him, to let him take the
burden from her. 'No wonder you looked so unhappy.
You identified with her because you still feel bad about
it, even after all this time, don't you?'

She nodded. 'It's strange, isn't it? You'd think I'd be
over it by now. Well, I am, of course, in a way. Life goes
on, and you learn to adjust—but I think it has affected
me badly overall, especially since...' She broke off.

'Since you split up with your ex?'

'I suppose so. I'm beginning to wonder if it's ever
possible to have a true and lasting relationship.' She
frowned. 'We'd been together for almost two years,
Ewan and I, and I'd actually begun to think we might
build a life together, but then it all started to go wrong.'

She gave a shuddery sigh. 'I don't even want to think
about it.'

'No, I can see that. Tell me more about your father.
Why does it still bother you so much?'

'I don't know. It was all so long ago, but when Mrs
Granger was talking, suddenly it was as though I was
back there, ten years old again. I could identify with
young Owen.' She was silent for a moment or two, her
mind dwelling on the past. 'It perhaps wouldn't have
been so bad if my father had kept in touch with us regu-

larly, but he didn't, and that hurt a lot. He went abroad for a while. He had this urge to see the world.' She sighed. 'I suppose now, when I think about it, it's more a feeling of sadness and frustration that comes over me because of the way he let us all down.'

'He let himself down.' His gaze met hers and deep down she knew he understood and was genuinely sympathetic towards her. And he had hit the nail on the head with his comment, hadn't he? Perhaps, for the first time, she realised why, even to this day, her father could never quite look her in the eye. He was ashamed of what he had done.

'Yes, I think you could be right.'

'Do you see him at all now?'

She nodded. 'Once in a while. Like I said, he was never very big on keeping in touch.'

Mrs Granger came back into the room just then, and he let his arm slip from her shoulders. Strangely, she instantly mourned the loss of it. It felt good to have him hold her, to be close to him and feel his strong body next to hers. He made her feel safe and she wanted him to go on holding her.

But perhaps it was just as well they had been interrupted. It wouldn't do for her to get too accustomed to having him near, would it? She might get to like it too much, and then she could end up hurt and disappointed all over again.

She edged away from the bedside and tried to remember that she was here to do a job of work. 'Did you manage to talk to your sister?' she asked the woman, and smiled when she nodded.

'She'll be with me in an hour or so.'

'That's good. I'm really pleased for you.' Jade started towards the door. 'I'll leave you to sit with Owen now but, as I said, I'll be back later this afternoon when I have some news.'

She glanced at Ben, wondering if he would stay behind, but he was already heading in her direction. 'I have to go down to A and E,' he said, checking his pager. He lowered his voice and added, 'Any time you want to talk to me, Jade, about anything at all, you only have to say.'

'Thanks. I appreciate that.'

She probably wouldn't do it, of course, though it was warming to know that he had offered. Her heart was telling her to go to him, to take comfort in him, but all the time her head was sounding an alarm. It rang, shrill and persistent, drowning out the yearnings of her weaker, feminine side.

She worked diligently for the rest of the day, grabbing a couple of hours of study time after attending a lecture in the main hall. Later in the afternoon she went back to the paediatric ward and sifted through the lab reports that had come in.

She collared Ben after he brought one of his patients back from a visit to Radiology. He was checking the X-ray films on the computer when she sought him out.

'I have Owen's test results from the lab,' she said. 'The blood tests show inflammation from an unknown source, and there are microscopic amounts of blood in his urine.'

'So it looks as though his kidneys are definitely involved in some way.' His dark brows drew together. 'Poor lad. We'll have to nip that in the bud.' He looked at her. 'This is good preparation for your final exams— do you recognise the illness?'

She nodded. 'Vasculitis, inflammation of the blood vessels. The rash is caused by bleeding under the skin.'

'Brilliant. As I recall, they're called Henoch Schönlein purpura.' Again those intelligent, grey-blue eyes studied her, and she just knew that one day he would be quizzing students like this in a regular way. 'And the treatment?'

'Steroids to settle the inflammation, along with im-munosuppressive drugs. And paracetamol to reduce pain and fever.'

He grinned. 'Top marks to Miss Blythe. Those hours of study are obviously paying off. Perhaps you can re-ward yourself with a few hours' break?'

'Yeah, right.' His grin was infectious. 'I've actually pulled out of my shift at the café bar tonight so that I can get some more time on the computer.'

He sucked his breath in through his teeth. 'You shouldn't work so hard. It'll tell on you in the end— you're already way too serious, and it seems to me you hardly ever take time out for fun. A night off will do you the world of good.'

She jabbed him in the chest with a finger. 'Says he, who wants to work really hard so that he's the best of the best of the best.' She thought about that for a sec-ond or two. 'And, of course, you will be, won't you, if you go around encouraging everyone else to slack?'

He laughed, clapping a hand to his head. 'Aargh. You found me out.'

She was still smiling when she left him a couple of minutes later. She went off to write up Owen's medication and present the chart to Professor Farnham for his signature.

'That's good work,' the professor said approvingly. 'And I see Ben has been conscientious in working with you. It looks as though you make a good team.'

Her eyes widened. Heaven forbid he should think of putting them together any more than they were already. How ever would she be able to function properly?

Jade thought about his comment as she finished her shift and headed for home. She liked working with Ben, there was no doubt about it, but it was playing havoc with her nerves. One look from those smoke-grey eyes and her whole body reacted as though he'd lit a fire in her. There'd be nothing left of her if it carried on.

The house was empty when she arrived home from work. That was unusual, and it felt really strange, but then she recalled that Lucy was out for the evening with her friends from Cardiology. They were celebrating because one of the girls had a birthday. And Matt had said he would be performing at a gig in a pub somewhere on the South Bank.

It meant that she had the house to herself for once, and for a little while she revelled in the sheer peace and quiet. She made herself something to eat, and then switched on her laptop and sat at the kitchen table to study a chapter on paediatric nephrology for an hour or so.

It was a subject that would most likely come up in her exams, but at the same time she was thinking about the little boy back at the hospital who was suffering from inflammation of his kidneys. It was horrible that the child's body could turn on itself and cause him so many problems, but at least they could do something to help him and ease his pain. With any luck it would only be a couple of weeks or so before he was back to his former self.

Eventually, she leaned back in her chair and stretched, easing her aching muscles. Perhaps Ben was right, and it would do her good to take a break. All at once, the idea of lying back in a warm bath filled with scented bubbles appealed to her more and more.

She closed the lid of the laptop and went upstairs to fill the tub. Then, after pinning up her hair into a silky topknot, and with the portable radio playing soothing, romantic music in the background, she soaked for half an hour, letting the warmth seep into her.

It was sheer bliss to simply do nothing for a change. She let the water flow luxuriously over her skin and watched the white foam form soft peaks all around her.

Unaccountably, her thoughts drifted to Ben. How did he relax at the end of the day? Ah, but he had his recliner, didn't he? A smile curved her lips as she imagined him stretched out on the supple leather, his long body moulded to the shape of the chair.

She shook the image away. No more thinking about Ben. It was altogether too unsettling.

She frowned as a soft clunking sound disturbed her peace. What was that? Had she left a window open somewhere, so that a gust of wind had knocked something over?

Everything was quiet once more, and she stepped out of the bath, drying herself and putting on fresh underwear and a towelling robe. She rubbed the condensation away from the mirror and saw that her face was pink and healthy looking, and damp strands of hair had escaped from the topknot to fall in wavy tendrils around her cheeks and throat.

There was that noise again…a clunk, clunk, clatter this time. Had Matt come home early from his gig? Perhaps it had been cancelled.

She turned off the radio and waited to find out if there were any more sounds, but there was only silence. Perhaps she had been imagining things. Most likely it was the cat from next door knocking plant pots over in the small garden.

She tidied up the bathroom and stepped out into the hallway. It was growing dusk by now, so she flicked on the light switch and a golden glow filled the landing.

'That's better. Why didn't I think of doing that?' Ben's voice broke the silence and she stared in disbelief as he came up the stairs towards her, carrying a large cardboard box filled with all kinds of paraphernalia. A skeleton's arm hung over the side, swinging to and fro as he advanced.

'Good heavens. You frightened the life out of me,' she said, her voice a little sharp edged because of the fright she'd just received. 'I thought I was alone in the house. And what's that?' She waved a hand at the collection of bones. 'I hope that thing isn't real.'

'Who? Freddie, do you mean?' He shook his head. 'He's harmless enough, I think—except when there's a full moon, that is. I try not to let him out on those occasions. I've had him for quite a while, and I'm really quite fond of him. I swiped him from the mortuary when no one was around.'

Her mouth dropped open in shock, until good sense got the better of her and she shook her head at him. 'As if!'

He gave her an impish grin, holding the box with one arm and lifting the skeleton's hand in a wave of greeting.

Recovering herself, she said curiously, 'What are you doing here, anyway? I thought you weren't supposed to be moving in until tomorrow.'

'My plans changed. I had the loan of the van earlier than expected—didn't Lucy tell you? My friend didn't need the van this evening after all, so I thought it would be better for me to bring my things over tonight. That way I have the whole weekend to settle in. I did let Lucy know about the change of plan this morning.'

'No, she didn't say anything.' Lucy had probably been in a rush, as usual, with a hundred and one items on her agenda, and it must have slipped her mind. Then again, she probably thought it wouldn't matter when he moved in.

He put down the box and then straightened up to look at her. 'Wow!' he said on a low whistle. 'Look at you. Now, there's an angel, if ever I saw one.' His gaze wandered over her. 'In my dreams I couldn't have conjured up such a sight to welcome me. Who would have thought it? I've come across the perfect vision of womanhood in a terraced house in the heart of London.'

'Oh, very funny,' she said crossly. She didn't know why she was out of sorts all of a sudden. He'd thrown her by being here, but that wasn't it. Maybe it was because he was so over the top in his comments that he had to be kidding, and she realised she didn't want him to be joking about the way she looked. Perverse, or what? Lucy would have simply smiled, accepting that she heard that kind of thing all the time.

He looked surprised. 'No, no... I mean it...every word. Really, I do.' Then she realised he was slowly coming towards her, his movements purposeful, his gaze fixed on her.

She took a step back, and clutched at her robe in case it should inadvertently slip open. 'S-stay where you are,' she told him warily. 'I think that's far enough.'

He stopped, and stayed perfectly still, heat flaring in the depths of his grey-blue eyes. 'Don't tell me you're afraid of me?' He seemed affronted by the idea. 'I thought you would have known me better than that.'

'I do. I'm not.' She didn't know why she was on the defensive. Perhaps the truth was that she was afraid of herself, afraid that if he came too close she would find herself drawn to him and before too long she'd be in way too deep for her peace of mind. 'I mean, I just... well, it doesn't matter... I wasn't expecting you, or I would have been dressed.'

His mouth curved as his glance drifted over her. 'Now, as far as I'm concerned, that would have been a real shame. I'm actually glad Lucy forgot to tell you...

because the truth is, no matter what you think, you do look absolutely gorgeous, with your baby-pink skin and those lovely green eyes firing sparks at me.'

She put up a hand as though to ward off his words. 'Okay, okay…let's call a halt now, shall we?'

He nodded. 'All right… If you're sure…if that's what you really want.'

'I am. It is.'

'It's just that I'd love to get to know you better, Jade…much better. I've a feeling you and I could be perfect together.'

She shook her head and stepped back from him, and only then did she realise that when she'd moved she'd inadvertently let go of the edges of the robe, and it slid open to reveal a glimpse of lace-edged underwear and a creamy expanse of thigh.

He sucked in his breath. Then, as he slowly exhaled, he said in a husky voice, 'Um…what was I saying? I seem to have lost the thread somehow.'

She pulled the robe tightly around her. 'Never mind. I think it's high time I left you to finish bringing in your stuff.'

She frowned, and began to edge towards her room. 'Any other time, I'd offer to give you a hand, but right now I'm going to put some clothes on. Then we'll start again, shall we, and pretend this never happened? I'll make coffee.'

He made a rueful smile. 'I'd far sooner explore where we might go from here.'

'No. Please, just forget it.' She gave a rueful smile and brushed past him to get to her room, but that turned out to be her biggest mistake. The slightest touch, the glide of his muscled arm against her body sent her senses reeling into chaos. She felt him react, his body stiffening as though he'd gone into shock. Her skin tingled, the blood fizzed in her veins, and heat surged through her from head to toe. She could feel her heart beginning to thud heavily, beating frantically against her chest wall.

She escaped into the sanctity of her room and closed the door behind her, leaning against the wood for a moment or two to catch her breath. How could she have deluded herself into thinking she was immune to him? His very nearness tantalised and teased her, and she had no idea at all what to do about it. He hadn't even moved in yet, and already she was struggling to keep her emotions in check.

CHAPTER FOUR

How was she going to get through the next few months unscathed? Jade fretted inwardly as she served tables at the café bar next day. It would be all too easy to get involved with Ben, but it would surely be disastrous for her. She wasn't ready to get entangled with any man.

And yet simply knowing that he was in the house was enough to make her feel feverish. Not just in the house, but actually in the room next to hers. She'd tossed and turned in her bed last night, hearing his movements through the wall that separated them.

And then, this morning, she'd helped him open boxes and move furniture about in his room, and she had been struck by how well they worked together, how much in tune with one another they seemed to be. There was an easy companionship between them…and something more, something indefinable that made her constantly aware of him, as though all her senses had been heightened.

Even Jacques had guessed that something was wrong. He studied her features suspiciously as she prepared to finish her shift. 'Why are you looking so pale, huh? Are you coming down with a virus or something?'

'No. No virus. It's nothing, Jacques,' she said. 'I've been studying a lot lately, that's all.' Though how she was going to get any work done with Ben around was beyond her imagining at the moment.

He looked at her again, unconvinced. 'It is only six o'clock on a Saturday afternoon. You should try getting some more sleep.' He shook his head. 'You young people…you never know when to stop, *c'est vrai*.'

She patted his shoulder. 'Thank you for worrying about me, Jacques, but I'm fine. I'll be here tomorrow morning, on time, as usual.'

He nodded, but as she collected her bag and jacket, he glanced at the door and said, 'Ah… I see it all now. *Voilà!*' He smiled as though everything had suddenly become clear to him. 'Man trouble. Always, there is a man.'

Jade frowned, following the direction of his gaze, and was startled to see Ben leaning negligently against the wall at the side of the door, one ankle crossed over the other. He was wearing casual clothes, jeans and a T-shirt that clung to his chest and showed off impressively broad shoulders. He looked at her, then straightened up, a half-smile playing over his lips, and for a second or two a wave of hot colour filled her cheeks. Just seeing him brought to mind their skirmish on the landing last night.

What was he doing here? He obviously hadn't come for a meal, or he would have gone over to a table.

'Go!' Jacques commanded her. 'On your way! He is waiting for you. This is what happens when you fall into a man's arms.'

'It isn't like that,' she muttered under her breath, embarrassed that he should bring up that occasion. One time she slipped, just one time, and she was never going to be allowed to forget it. 'You have totally the wrong idea.'

'Hah!' Her boss shook his head in disbelief.

Ben met her as she went to the door. 'Hi,' he said. 'I thought I'd come and walk you home—as a sort of thank-you for helping me to move the desk and so on and for making me breakfast this morning.'

He placed his hand gently beneath her elbow and ushered her out of the door. 'It was nothing,' she murmured. 'I was already up, and making breakfast for myself, so it was no trouble for me to add a couple more eggs to the omelette.'

'Even so, it was thoughtful of you to take the trouble, especially as you were running to a tight schedule. I really appreciated what you did.'

They walked out into the evening sunshine and Jade glanced at him fleetingly. Despite her reservations, it felt surprisingly good to have him here beside her, tall and strong, taking the trouble to match his long stride to hers. It hadn't occurred to her before to worry too much about walking through the streets of London alone, but with him beside her she immediately felt safe and secure.

'Have you managed to sort yourself out?' she asked. 'Have you arranged everything as you like it?' That morning he had been surrounded by boxes and furniture and bits and pieces, and it amazed her that he could have managed to accumulate so much stuff in such a short time.

'Not quite. The room is fairly large but I'm having a bit of a problem fitting everything in.' He smiled. 'I'll get there in the end, I'm sure.' He sent her a sideways glance. 'Perhaps you could advise me on layout. I've tried a couple of options but so far they're not working out too well.'

She nodded. 'You have some good pieces of furniture,' she acknowledged. 'It's a bit unusual, really. Mostly, when students move around, they tend to be wary of accumulating a lot of stuff that has to be taken with them wherever they go.'

'I know, but I like having familiar things around me. It helps me to settle in, and I find I can study much better when I'm comfortable.' He laid a hand in the small of her back as he guided her around tables and chairs that had been set out on the pavement at a café further along the road, and a wonderful sensation of warmth rippled along her spine and spread out across her hips.

'The desk belonged to my grandfather, and it's really special to me,' he was saying. 'I thought the world of him, and he encouraged me tremendously when he knew I wanted to go to medical school. He was a doctor himself, a brilliant man, and when I sit at the desk I often think of him and what he achieved. I'm not at all sure I'll be able to live up to his example, but I'll definitely do my best.'

So that explained why he was so ambitious. His grandfather had something to do with it.

They passed by a pub where the glass doors had

been opened wide to let in the fresh air, and the throb of music livened the atmosphere. She said thoughtfully, 'Did the leather recliner belong to him as well? I noticed both that and the desk are in very good condition.'

He nodded. 'It came from his study. They've been cherished over the years. I remember often seeing my grandmother and my mother rub them with furniture polish.' His mouth curved and she guessed he was seeing it once more in his mind's eye. 'All the other stuff is what I've acquired as I've gone through medical school...the desk lamp, filing cabinet and the bookshelf with the set of medical books. They're all things I wouldn't want to be without.'

They turned off the main street into a much quieter area made up of housing interspersed with business units. 'What about you?' he asked. 'Have you brought anything with you from home?'

She made a wry face. 'There wasn't a great deal left, after my older brothers took what they wanted. They both have their own places now—James is living in a bachelor flat, and Tom is married and has bought a house back home in Amersham. Neither of them had much money to set up house, so my mother did what she could, giving them things she didn't really need any more.'

'And your younger brother, Ross?'

'He's a student—studying horticulture. He's not really interested in material things. He likes wide, open spaces and anything to do with nature.'

By now they had reached the leafy crescent that was their home. Jade breathed in the delicate scent of cherry blossom and smiled. 'I love this time of year, when everything is full of colour and you know that summer is just around the corner.' She frowned. 'Except for exams looming, of course.'

He pulled a face. 'That *is* a bit of a downer, I'll grant you. But I'm sure you'll do fine. You always seem very capable and in control.'

'Do I?' She wasn't convinced she always felt that way, but she said, 'Thanks for that.' She unlocked the front door, and sniffed the air once more as she entered the hallway. 'Is that pizza I can smell?' She gave a wide smile, her spirits instantly lifted.

'I think it is.' Ben smiled with her. 'Apparently it's Matt's turn to cook. I wasn't sure whether that was a good or bad thing. I know when it's my turn, you'll all have to get used to simple stuff like pasta or fry-ups.'

'Sounds okay to me—I'll eat pretty much anything. Mind you, I can't see Lucy going for many fries—she doesn't keep that figure by pigging out on cream cakes and burgers, you know.'

'Hmm. It looks as though I'll have to have a rethink.' His glance shifted over her, sliding along the length of her jeans-clad legs. 'You must burn off everything that you eat.' He smiled. 'You look gorgeous, with curves in all the right places. It doesn't look as though there's an ounce of fat on you.'

She gave him a mildly sceptical glance. It wasn't entirely true, but she couldn't help a small thrill of delight that he thought so.

He turned in the direction of the stairs. 'You go and

sort yourself out some pizza. I have something I need to do, but I'll be down in a minute or two.'

'Okay.' Jade went into the kitchen and draped her jacket over the back of a chair before going to wash her hands at the sink. 'That smells really good,' she told Matt, who was looking pleased with himself as he cut a huge pizza into separate portions.

'Yes, I think I've surpassed expectations this time, if I say so myself,' he said with a grin. 'It's the seasoning, and the mushrooms and peppers that make all the difference, you know.' He glanced around. 'Is our new housemate coming to join us?'

'I'm here,' Ben acknowledged, walking into the room. He was carrying the skeleton, and for a moment Lucy stared at it, looking nonplussed. She'd been laying out cutlery on the large pine table, but now she simply stood, as though transfixed.

'What's that?' she asked.

'You mean, who is that?' Jade said. 'His name's Freddie. Perhaps he's come to have supper with us?'

Matt laughed. 'Of course. We should have guessed. Why don't you set a place for him at the table, Lucy? He's quite skinny, so I doubt he'll eat too much.'

Ben chuckled, but then became uncharacteristically hesitant for a moment or two. 'I…um…I wondered if it would be all right if I could find a place for him in the living room?' he ventured, looking at Lucy. 'I've tried every which way to fit him into the bedroom, but I'm running out of space upstairs.'

Lucy tried her best not to smile. 'A skeleton in the living room?' She shook her head. 'I'm sorry, but I really don't think we want him down here. After all, this is our home. If we start bringing things like that into the living room, it'll soon begin to look more like a junk shop than anything else.'

'I understand how you feel, but he'll be no trouble at all, honestly,' Ben said in a coaxing tone. 'I could hide him in a corner. He only gets bothersome if you try to get too close, then he's all over you. Can't keep his hands still, you see.' He moved Freddie in close to his body, and the skeleton's long arms wrapped themselves around him.

Lucy smiled. 'Even so…' She turned to Jade. 'What do you think?'

Jade winced. 'I kind of agree,' she said regretfully. 'It's a bit like keeping bikes in the hallway. Once you start that kind of thing, it gathers momentum, and before you know it, you find yourself surrounded by clutter. That's why we made a rule about it.' She glanced at Matt, and his mouth turned down in a rueful grimace. 'Believe me, with three brothers, I know what I'm talking about. Besides, I don't always want to be reminded of work when I'm trying to relax at the end of the day. And with Freddie around, you can't help but think of much else, can you?'

'Perhaps we should put it to the vote,' Matt suggested. He lifted his hand in the air. 'I'm all for it.' He started to count hands. 'One, two…' He broke off and started to laugh when he saw that Freddie's hand was raised and waving optimistically. Ben gave them all a hopeful smile, his eyes wide and innocent.

'Three. That's three in favour,' Matt said.

'No, no…that's not allowed,' Lucy said, chuckling in spite of herself. 'And, anyway, it's actually a draw, so I'm sorry, but I think we should take that as a no.'

'Would that be a definite no? Not a maybe, or a possibly…?' Ben appeared suitably crushed.

'Sorry.' Lucy was adamant.

'How would it be if I found him a place on the landing upstairs? He'd fit very well into the corner, and it's quite a wide landing.'

'Oh, no. Definitely not,' Jade said firmly. 'There's absolutely no way I'm climbing the stairs in the middle of the night when I'm tired and not thinking too clearly and risking bumping into a skeleton.'

'Oh, I don't know.' He gave her a wicked smile. 'It might be quite romantic in the moonlight, getting into a clinch.'

She knew he was thinking about the previous night and she went hot all over. 'Heaven forbid.' She was thoughtful for a second or two. 'Tell you what—why don't I go with you after we've eaten and see if there's any way we can reorganise your room? I'm sure we'll be able to come up with something.'

'Okay. That sounds like a good idea.' Ben perched Freddie on a chair and took a seat next to him.

Jade sat down and started to tuck into a pizza slice. 'Did Freddie belong to your grandfather?'

He nodded. 'He was with him through all the time he was studying for exams, and later on he always took part in lectures when my grandfather taught anatomy.'

'Where is your grandfather now?' Lucy asked. 'Is he still lecturing?'

'No.' His voice softened. 'He died three years ago, unfortunately.' A look of sadness crossed his face briefly, but then he reverted to his normal self and added, 'He lived to a grand old age, though, so I suppose I should be glad of that. He was a great man—a bit disappointed that my father went into business, rather than medicine, but he was thrilled to bits when I took it up.'

'I'm sorry. But, like you say, it's wonderful to have grandparents live to a ripe old age.' Lucy took a bite from her pizza and became thoughtful. 'This is actually quite good,' she murmured, savouring the taste. She tried another bite. 'Mmm…not bad at all.'

'You don't have to sound so surprised,' Matt said gruffly. 'Pizza's one of my specialities.'

'Yes, well, I didn't mean… Okay, you're a good cook, all right?' She conceded defeat, and Matt smirked.

'Better than you, anyway.'

Lucy bridled. 'Are you insinuating that I can't cook?' she demanded. 'I'll have you know that the last meal I prepared was from a gourmet recipe. A lot of fine ingredients went into it, and after all the time I spent on the preparation, what did you have to say about it, huh? Quote, "I can't be doing with fancy food."'

They went on arguing while Jade finished off her meal and wiped her hands on a piece of kitchen towel. She glanced at Ben. 'If you've finished, shall we go up and take a look at your room? We might as well leave these two to get on with it—they can go on for ages sometimes.'

Ben grinned, and nodded. He gathered up Freddie, and followed her up the stairs.

Jade looked around his room. With all his stuff in there it looked overwhelmingly cluttered. 'Hmm. It doesn't look quite right, does it? Perhaps you ought to ask Lucy if she'd mind having the table downstairs. There's room for it in the hall, and she could always pretty it up with a vase of flowers and a few ornaments. I think she might go for that. Then you could put the filing cabinet next to the desk with the lamp on top of it, and you'll be able to have one half of the room purely for office-type things. And there'll be room for the recliner over there in the corner, with Freddie on the other side of the desk.'

He looked at her with renewed respect. 'You're good, aren't you?' he said. 'Very good. So good, in fact, that I think you deserve a hug.'

And then, before she had any inkling of what he planned to do, he had wrapped his arms around her and was drawing her close. 'I knew I could rely on you,' he said, smiling down at her.

She wanted to return the smile, but she was too busy fighting off all the bewildering new sensations that were besieging her. His hands were resting on the base of her spine, while her body was crushed against his, and she was overwhelmingly conscious of the softness of her curves melding with the hard contours of his masculine frame.

She struggled to clear her head as the warmth from those hands permeated her flesh and carried delicious messages of sensual pleasure along various pathways.

'I think you may be getting a bit ahead of yourself,' she said, trying to keep her voice steady, while her heart was pounding out a heavy, rhythmic beat. 'You still have to get Lucy to agree to it.'

'Oh, that shouldn't be too much of a problem, should it? I can see why she might not want Freddie to grace the living area but, like you say, an elegant piece of furniture wouldn't go amiss, would it? I'm pretty sure I'll be able to talk her round.' His hands strayed to the curve of her hips, lingering there and filling her with a strange kind of yearning.

'Hmm. Yes, I expect you will.'

He lowered his head so that his lips lightly brushed her cheek, and a fluttery sensation started up in her chest. Tempting as it was to stay in his arms, she knew she had to break it off before things got out of hand. Laying her palm against his chest, she gently pushed him away. 'Perhaps you should go and tackle her about it now,' she said huskily. 'I expect she'll be glad of the interruption after she and Matt have been sparring for a while. You'll win out through simply not being Matt.'

He laughed, and studied her for a moment or two, his arms still around her. 'And there I was just beginning to enjoy getting you in a clinch. Maybe we could do it again some time?'

She smiled sweetly. 'Don't push your luck.'

'No? Well, if kisses and cuddles are out, what if I try a different tack? I was going to ask if you'd come along with me to the medical school's charity event next weekend. We go out with collecting tins to see how much money we can raise. Would that be taking things too far?'

'Um…no, of course not.' She tried to think things through, still hungry for the embrace she'd denied herself. 'I mean, Matt and Lucy will be going along, too, won't they?' It wasn't as though it would be just the two of them, and that would be a far safer way of spending time with him, wouldn't it? She felt a tug of excitement, immediately tempered by caution. 'I don't know if it will be possible, though,' she murmured. 'I have to work at the café bar.'

'Ask for some time off.'

'I'll try, but I might not be able to manage it. The bar gets busy at weekends.'

He sighed, bending his head so that his cheek rested against hers. 'That would be an awful shame,' he murmured. 'I'd love to spend time with you.' Then he straightened and reluctantly eased himself away from her, and she immediately began to wage war within herself. Why couldn't she simply relax and enjoy the luxury of being in his arms? But she knew the answer. The minute she gave in to her feelings and allowed herself to be swayed by his masculine charm, she laid herself open to hurt and disillusion.

So instead she left him to go and sort things out with Lucy, and went to her room to catch up on her studies. Or at least that was what she meant to do, but as soon as she switched on the laptop and stared at the medical text, all her concentration flew out of the window. All she could think of was Ben.

Next morning, when she went downstairs to grab

breakfast before setting off for work at the café bar, she wasn't at all surprised to see the fine mahogany table from Ben's room gracing the hallway. Lucy had even managed to find an ornate letter rack and a beautiful set of wrought-iron candleholders, which now had pride of place on the polished surface.

She didn't see anything of Ben for the rest of the day. When she finished work at the café bar, she was half expecting, half hoping that he would be there to walk her home again, but it didn't happen, and she resigned herself to walking home alone. He probably had other things to do with his time. Why would he choose to single her out all the while, especially if she persisted in being less than encouraging towards him?

Then, when she arrived at the house, she learned from Lucy that he'd left earlier that day to go and visit his family in Hampshire, a drive of around an hour and a half each way.

'He won't be back until late this evening.' Lucy sighed. 'He's lovely, isn't he? So easy to talk to, and such a great sense of humour. You're so lucky to be working with him every day.'

'Yes, I suppose I am.'

Lucy raised her eyes heavenwards. 'Lord, Jade. Talk about damning with faint praise. How can you be so casual about him? I'd swap places with you any day.'

'Sure you would. Then you wouldn't have to deal with that nice Mr Sheldon, who keeps you so busy in cardiology.'

'Oh—no, don't remind me. I have to do a presentation for him tomorrow. Eek!'

* * *

They set off for the hospital after breakfast next morning and there was still no sign of either Ben or Matt. Jade had heard Ben come in late the previous night, though, to be fair to him, he'd crept about so as not to wake anyone, and it was only because she had been sleeping fitfully that she'd heard him. That morning both men must have made an early start.

Ben was leafing through a batch of lab test results when Jade walked onto the ward an hour or so later. He looked up as she approached and gave her a brief smile, then returned to studying the forms as Mandy greeted her.

'We're admitting a six-year-old-girl,' Mandy said. 'She was brought in to A and E in the early hours of the morning and they've transferred her to us.'

'Oh, I see.'

Ben finished with the forms and put them back in the tray. 'Thanks, Mandy. We'll keep the child on oxygen and monitor her heart rate and breathing. I'm going to prescribe a stronger antibiotic to be given intravenously and we'll get a chest X-ray. I've written out the forms for further tests.'

'Okay, I'll see to it.' Mandy was a good-looking woman, with a wide, perfectly shaped mouth and high cheekbones. Her eyes were a clear grey, and she had long, fair hair that was fastened with a clip at the back of her head.

She went off to deal with the matters in hand, and Ben turned to Jade. 'Hi, there. I was sorry I missed you yesterday and this morning. And we don't even have time to catch up properly now, because we need to see to young Katie. She's in a bad way.'

He took her over to the bedside, where a small girl lay back, propped up against the white pillows, fighting for breath. The monitors were bleeping, showing a rapid heart rate, fast respiration and a low blood-oxygen level. It was distressing to see her this way.

Her parents were sitting by her side, their faces drawn with anxiety. Ben pulled up a chair and spoke to them calmly. 'At the moment, Katie's just about holding her own, but we may need to put a tube down her throat to assist her breathing if things change. It's possible that she has bacterial pneumonia, but we'll know more when we get the results of specific tests. In the meantime, we're treating her with strong antibiotics and making sure that she has a steady flow of oxygen.'

He looked from one to the other. 'Is there anything you would like to ask me?'

The mother nodded. 'Can I stay with her? I mean, all the time, every day.'

'Yes, of course. The nurse will show you a room where you can sleep, and there's a table set out with snacks so that you can help yourself. These things happen out of the blue, and you aren't always prepared.' He smiled. 'So, if there's anything you need, just ask. Mandy will be glad to help.'

They spoke for a little while longer, and then Ben checked the monitors once more. 'We need to make sure that she gets plenty of fluids,' he told the parents, 'so the nurse will pour drinks for her from a measured jug—we have to keep a check on how much she's getting, so if you refill the jug, let Mandy know.'

They nodded, and he took his leave of them, walking over to the office with Jade. 'Do you want to follow up on this one for your assessment file?' he asked. 'I noticed you looked concerned, and that you were looking at her chart while I was talking to the parents.' He shut the office door and went to sit down at the computer. Jade perched herself on the edge of the desk.

She nodded. 'It's upsetting seeing a child struggling to breathe like that. I remember when it happened to my brother when he was small. It was very scary.'

'He had pneumonia?' He started to key his notes into the computer.

'Yes. We were all really worried about him. My mother had so much to deal with back then, being a single mother with four children, and when Ross became ill she was beside herself. Well, you can imagine.'

He nodded. 'Did your father come back to see Ross?'

'Yes. We hoped he and my mother would get back together after that, but the marriage was over. He'd had affairs through the years, and finally my mother got tired of it and divorced him.'

He winced. 'I suppose things must be easier for her now, with everyone off her hands.'

'Yes. Actually, she married again about a year before I went off to medical school.' She smiled. 'I was glad for Mum but, to be honest, they were so wrapped up in one another, I was glad to get away.'

He grinned. 'I can't imagine what it must have been

like to be one of four children. I expect, as the only girl, you must have been cherished.'

She made a wry face. 'I'm sure I was, but the truth of it is my mother had to spend most of her time sorting out the boys. They were always up to something. Always teasing me and falling out with one another, and causing bother of some sort. It goes with the territory, I suppose.' She laughed. 'I love them all dearly, but I'm quite glad they're grown up now. Well, Ross still has some way to go, but he's getting there, slowly.'

She studied him thoughtfully for a moment or two, taking in his strong, sculpted features, the confident, easy manner that was natural to him. Had he once been a teenage tearaway? She couldn't imagine it.

'So how did things go with your family yesterday?' she asked. 'Lucy said you went down to Hampshire for the day.'

'Oh, it was great. It was my mother's birthday. My sister was over there with her husband and their two children, and we all had lunch together at a country pub. Then we spent the afternoon wandering around the quayside.'

'It sounds like bliss.'

He nodded. 'Maybe it's the sort of thing you should be doing more often. There's more to life than work and study, you know.'

She rolled her eyes. 'Yeah, I know. Chance would be a fine thing.'

'I'd be happy to oblige.' His glance travelled over her, from the smooth, burnished chestnut of her hair, along the gentle contours outlined by the cotton shirt she was wearing, nipped in at the waist and flaring out over her pencil-slim skirt, and then shimmered down over her long, shapely legs. 'More than happy.'

'Well, thank you for that,' she murmured. 'I'll give it some thought.'

Not that anything would happen in a month of Sundays. She had far too much to do, and if she had any sense at all, she'd run from him as fast as she could go.

His eyes glinted. 'I really wish you'd do more than give it some thought, Jade. Somehow, I get the feeling you're busy putting up barriers as fast as I try to tear them down.'

CHAPTER FIVE

'HE'S losing consciousness. I'm afraid we may have to alert the intensive care unit if he goes any further downhill.'

Ben's expression was serious, and Jade could see that he was deeply affected by the plight of their young patient—but there was something else in his manner that gave her pause for thought. As usual, he had complete command of the situation, and his every action confirmed that without doubt he was an excellent doctor. There were no probationary nerves, no hesitancy, just confident and capable application of all the skills he had learned over these last few years...and yet, in spite of all that, there was something about him that made her suspect that deep down he was troubled.

'What's happening to my son? Why is he breathing like that and not answering? Is he going to be all right?' The boy's mother had come in to hospital with her child by ambulance, and she was obviously agitated and frightened. Now she laid a hand on Jade's arm, her eyes pleading with her. 'They didn't tell me much down in A and E, but then they said he needed to be admitted. What's going to happen to him?'

Jade glanced at Ben and he indicated with a slight nod of his head that she should take her to one side.

She felt a comforting warmth start up inside her with the knowledge that he trusted her to explain to the woman everything that was going on. 'Shall we go and sit down over there?' Jade pointed to a chair to one side of the treatment room, and when the woman was settled she pulled up another chair beside her. She sat down and spoke calmly, doing her best to soothe her.

Her son was twelve years old, and he had been vomiting for several hours before admission. His breathing was deep and sighing—a strange and frightening sound—and his heart rate was rapid. His condition was worrying to everyone, not just his mother.

'They've put him on a drip. That means it's serious, doesn't it?' Mrs Sumner was very agitated.

Jade tried to reassure her. 'Jason is on a drip because he's dehydrated, and we have to put that right.'

'Oh, I see.' The woman frowned. 'He's not been well for a couple of weeks, and I thought all this was something to do with his chest problems...but he has diabetes, too. Could this collapse be something to do with that?'

Jade nodded. 'It's probably a combination of things. The tests we've done so far show that his blood sugar is high and his blood is becoming more acidic, so we need to correct both of those conditions as soon as possible. It's most likely caused by a shortage of insulin.'

'But how—why is his blood more acid?' Mrs Sumner seemed bewildered.

'The shortage of insulin causes the body to burn off

excess fat, and that leads to the production of acidic ketones. Jason's deep, sighing way of breathing is his body's way of trying to compensate for the acidity by blowing off carbon dioxide.'

'Oh, I see.' She frowned. 'And giving him fluids will put things right?'

Jade nodded. 'That's the beginning of his treatment.' She glanced across the room to where Ben was treating the boy. He had organised urgent blood and urine cultures for the lab, and was setting up an infusion of insulin. And all the while he was tense, his whole body stiff and on the alert.

'Dr Langley is giving him insulin right now, and hopefully Jason will start to get better from here on.' She looked at the woman, seeing some of the tension ease from her features. She was sitting on the edge of her seat, peering anxiously at her son, prompting Jade to say softly, 'Would you like to go and sit by his bedside? If you have any more questions, you only have to ask. The nurse will always be available to help you if I'm not around.'

'Thank you.'

Ben spoke quietly to the woman for a while, and then when he had done all he could for the boy, he came over to Jade.

'His potassium level is low, which could explain the heart irregularities. I've added it to the intravenous infusion.'

'And the antibiotics? I noticed you'd prescribed them. Does he have some sort of infection?'

'I think so, especially after seeing the initial blood

test results. His mother said he'd been unwell for the last week, and that could be what's brought all this on.' He turned his head to look at the monitors once more and appeared to relax a little. 'His heart rate has slowed a bit. At least that's a good sign.'

'You seem to be very worried about him.' It was clear to her, if not to the boy's mother, that he was disturbed by the child's condition, and that was a bit baffling. He was never fazed by the assortment of conditions he had to treat—serious or not so serious, he always seemed to have the solution at his fingertips. 'Is there something about his case that concerns you more than usual?'

'Not especially. After all, we're doing everything that needs to be done.' Seeing she was still unconvinced, he added quietly, 'Children like Jason are the reason I came into medicine.'

'Really?' She studied him keenly, seeing the sincerity in his eyes. 'Do you mean that you wanted to specialise in his particular type of illness?'

'No, it was more that I knew someone who had the same condition.' He frowned. 'My friend's young sister collapsed on the kitchen floor at his house one day. It was terrifying. His parents were out somewhere, and we were just teenagers… I was seventeen…and neither of us had a clue what to do. I called for an ambulance, and then I remembered my grandfather, so I phoned him and he told me how to go on. He arrived before the paramedics, though, and managed to bring her round.' His mouth flattened. 'I had so much respect for him that day. I thought how marvellous it was that he could save lives.'

Jade studied his strong, tormented features. She could imagine that teenage boy, scared and at a loss. The girl's illness must have made a profound impression on him because even now he was disturbed by the memory. 'I can see why your grandfather would have been proud of you, wanting to take up medicine.'

He made a wry face. 'Well, maybe in the last few years. I think I gave everyone a few grey hairs before that.' He moved back to the bedside and Jade watched him go. She was puzzled. What had he meant by that last remark? Surely his family must always have been proud of him? She couldn't relate the man she knew to any kind of hothead.

Ben's pager bleeped and he gave her a regretful look as he went to answer it. 'I expect I'll see you later.'

She nodded. Her stomach was rumbling, reminding her that she hadn't eaten since breakfast, and now it was way past time for her lunch break. She went over to the staff lounge and rummaged in the fridge for the snack she had brought with her from home. There was only one other person in the room with her, a junior doctor who she'd known since her early days as a student.

'That looks good. What is it, quiche?' Greg was making tea, and after a nod from Jade he filled her cup for her.

'Cheese and bacon quiche.' She grinned. 'Yum.'

Greg smiled with her. He was a good-looking man, with strong angular features, and dark hair that was cut in a short, youthful style. He'd helped her through her break-up with Ewan, sympathising when she was upset and offering a brotherly shoulder to lean on. They were simply friends—his fiancée worked in a hospital across town.

'Is that a sample of your cooking?' he asked now.

She shook her head. 'Don't I wish? Matt made it last night, along with the salad I have here. Luckily, he made more than enough.' She sliced off a piece and handed it to him. 'Here, have a taste.'

'Hmm...this is good.' Greg nodded, taking another bite. 'Does Matt do all the cooking?'

'No, we all take turns. It's all mostly basic stuff. We're nearly always pushed for time, so there's nothing really fancy—Ben often says he misses things like real home-made puddings and cakes and so on, but if we do have something for dessert we usually make do with whatever we can buy cheap off the shelf.'

They ate together in silence, appreciating the subtle flavours and light texture of the tart.

Then Jade noticed a copy of the students' magazine lying on the table, and she picked it up and began to flick through it, while Greg leafed through a medical journal. There were several interesting articles in Jade's magazine, to do with student finance or advice on upcoming exams, and there was a piece on the charity event that was to take place this coming weekend. The students would be going out and about with collecting tins, hoping to tempt people into giving generously for various good causes.

She turned the page to discover a cartoon that Ben had drawn. She began to chuckle.

'What's funny?' Greg came to look over her shoulder. Then, as he took in the captions and saw the caricature of the skeleton, he began to smile. 'I remember you telling me about Freddie, the new addition to the household.'

'And here he is again,' she said, 'with his nose well and truly out of joint because he's been relegated to a poky desk under the stairs. From the looks of those piles of books that surround him, he seems to have worn himself down to the bone with studying.'

'While everyone else is having fun at the charity ball.' Greg read out the caption. 'Exam-time blues—everybody gets to party but me.'

He laughed and put his arm around Jade's shoulder. 'It's good to see you smiling again,' he said. 'You know, I was worried about you for quite a while after that useless nobody let you down. I couldn't see how you might put the sparkle back into your life, but I think perhaps you're getting there, bit by bit.'

She nodded. 'I try not to think about him any more.' She looked up at him. 'I know I thanked you for the way you put up with me and my moods back then, but I'm saying it again. You were great.'

The door to the staff lounge opened, but for a moment neither of them turned to see who had come into the room. Greg lightly squeezed her shoulder, and then moved away from her, and Jade glanced towards the door.

Ben was there, frowning, looking from her to Greg and back again, his eyes dark, his expression unreadable.

'Is everything all right—is Jason okay?' Jade asked, though she didn't think his grim mood had anything at all to do with his patients. He'd seen Greg with his arm around her, and he was drawing conclusions, but maybe it would be best for her to go on as if everything was normal.

He took a moment to answer, and then said, 'Yes, he appears to be doing all right.'

'Good. I grabbed the chance to go and take a look at Katie in the next bay, earlier on. She appears to be a lot better today. Her blood oxygen level's up, and her breathing's much easier.'

He nodded. 'She seems to be a lot more comfortable.'

Greg went over to the sink and rinsed his cup. 'See you later,' he said, and walked out into the corridor.

Jade stood up and began to clear away her lunch things.

'So what was all that about?' Ben asked, his glance moving over her. 'That business just now with Greg.'

She frowned. 'I don't know what you mean.'

'I think you do.' His mouth twisted impatiently. 'He had his arm around you. Is there something going on between you two?'

'No, nothing at all. Greg and I go way back, and he's always been a good friend to me. He was there for me when I broke up with Ewan and he made time to listen to me when I was upset.'

His eyes darkened. 'I want to be there for you. I see that you're hurting and still reacting to what happened, but you don't talk about it, and you push me away. I need you to let me in, Jade. I care about you—you must know that. I want to help.'

Had she been wrong to shut him out? She felt a lump

forming in her throat. 'It's been difficult for me to confide in anyone,' she told him. 'It's different with Greg,
because he's not interested in me romantically—he already has a girlfriend. But you want something from
me, and I'm not sure I can give you what you want.'
She laid a hand on his arm. 'You have to understand
that I've been hurt, badly, and I don't want to go there
again.'

Ben's arms went around her. 'I'd never hurt you,' he
said softly. 'You have to believe me.'

'I'd like to, but it's not that easy.' She swallowed.
'I trusted Ewan, you see. I thought I was in love with
him, and he with me, but he began to get restless...
He was already qualified as a doctor, and he started to
talk about going to work overseas, in South America.
I didn't want to go there. I have my family here, and I
felt that this is where I belong.'

She hesitated, thinking about that horrible time when
her world had started to fall apart. 'He started to let me
down, not turning up when he'd said he would, and he
became evasive. He kept telling me he loved me, but I
found out later that he was seeing someone else, one of
the junior doctors. I confronted him about it, and then
he told me he was going to Argentina to work for a
year.' Her voice quivered. 'We broke up, and later on I
learned that Marianne, the doctor, had gone with him.'

Ben's arms tightened on her. He seemed angry. 'It
seems to me that you're better off without him. He
treated you badly and you deserve much better than
that.'

She made a weak smile. 'That's what I keep telling myself. He walked out on me—well, I told him to go—but it was a huge shock to my system. It seemed as though one minute he was here with me, and we were happy, and the next he was half a world away. Though he did keep in touch occasionally, sending me texts from various places.'

She frowned. In a way it seemed odd that he'd kept up that contact with her, but perhaps Ewan had simply wanted to remain friends. 'Anyway...' she straightened, drawing in a deep breath '...I'm over him now. I'm just afraid to dip my toes in the water again for fear of the same thing happening to me. When Ewan left, it felt as though I'd been punched in the stomach, the same way it felt when my father left and didn't come back—well, not for a long time, at least. I'd been abandoned all over again... I was unloved and maybe I was unlovable.'

'Never.' Ben dropped a light kiss on her forehead. 'You can't go on like this, Jade. Sometimes you have to face up to what's troubling you, take a chance. Are you going to hide away all your life...never experience joy because you're scared that things might go wrong?'

'I don't know. I don't know what to do.' She looked up at him. 'I'm very confused.'

'That's natural.' He lowered his head and brushed his lips over hers in a kiss that was so light she thought she might have imagined it. And yet her lips were tingling, almost as though they were clamouring for more. 'Let me show you how to go on,' he murmured.

He kissed her again, tenderly, lovingly, as though she was the most precious thing in all the world to him. His lips caressed, coaxed and teased, so that her mouth softened beneath his and she clung to him, glad to be in his arms, and wanting everything that he had to offer.

But even now, in the back of her mind, she was uncertain. Was he right? Ought she to make that leap in the dark? Could she bear it if he let her down?

She heard footsteps outside in the corridor, and Ben must have heard them too because he reluctantly eased back from her.

'Why don't you make a fresh start, and take a chance on life?' he suggested softly. 'You could come to the dance with me on Friday—the charity disco at the student union bar. Matt will be playing in the band.'

Someone walked into the room then, another of the fifth-year students, and Jade nodded acknowledgement. It gave her a second or two to think things through. 'I'm supposed to be working at the café bar,' she told Ben, her voice quiet. 'I could perhaps go in for a couple of hours and ask Jacques for rest of the time off.'

'Good. That's the spirit.'

By the time Friday came around, though, she was already beginning to regret her hasty decision. It was surely a mistake to give Ben too much encouragement, because she didn't want him to read too much into it.

'Why on earth are you worrying?' Lucy said, shaking her head. 'Go out and enjoy yourself. I'll be there with Alice and Mandy and a couple of fifth-year students. It'll be a good night.' She lowered her voice to a conspiratorial whisper. 'Although I wouldn't say it in front of him, Matt plays a mean guitar, and the band is great. We'll have a fantastic time. And we could all do with a break after the hard work we've put in these last few months.'

Jade nodded. 'You're right. I don't know why I'm hesitating. I could do with a night out, and if we're all together, things should turn out well, shouldn't they?'

She dressed carefully for the evening, in black tights, overlaid with a short skirt and a pretty, glittery top. Her newly washed hair fell in a silky swathe to below her shoulders. She kept a light touch with her make-up and finished off with a bright lipstick that showed off her nicely shaped, full lips, and finally she was satisfied that she looked okay.

She checked her watch and went downstairs.

'I really like that—a woman who gets ready on time.' Ben's voice startled her and she turned to see him walk into the living room. His eyes darkened as his gaze moved slowly over her, a smoky, burning lick of flame. 'And you look lovely, absolutely gorgeous.'

She looked at him in return. Dressed all in black— black shirt, black trousers—he was incredibly sexy and her heart began to thump heavily.

'It was a bit of a rush after doing a stint at the café bar,' she said. 'But I didn't want to miss anything. I'm looking forward to hearing Matt play.' She smiled. 'It's not quite the same, hearing him belt out numbers from his room.'

'True.' His glance moved over her once more, as though he couldn't get enough of her. 'It sounds as though there'll be quite a crowd going to see him. My friend Jack will be there. Do you remember him from the café?'

'Toasted cheese sandwich, no expense spared, seems to ring a bell.' She laughed ruefully. 'I tend to remember customers by their orders. Quite often they'll have the same thing each time they visit.'

He chuckled. 'That's one way to do it.' Lucy came into the room just then, and they set off for the students' union bar together.

Jade looked around, drinking in the warm atmosphere, the comfy leather-covered seating and the sound of laughter and people chatting. The lighting was subdued, but moonlight shimmered through the room because one wall was completely made of glass.

There were tables dotted around the dance floor, and while Lucy and Jack claimed two of these for the group, the others went up to the bar to fetch drinks.

They talked for a while, and then the band started up and people streamed onto the dance floor. Jade and Ben joined them, moving to the rhythm of the music, along with their friends, and waving at Matt at the same time. There was no doubt about it, he was a very good musician.

After a while, when she murmured that she was thirsty and ready for a break, Ben handed her a glass of sparkling wine, and they slipped away from the group, to go and look at the view of London through the magnificent wall of glass.

'It's impressive, isn't it?' Ben stood beside her, sliding an arm around her waist.

'It is. It's spectacular, especially with all the buildings lit up near the waterfront and in the distance.'

Below them, the Thames glittered, a wide, meander-
ing ribbon of water threading its way through London.
In the distance, the great circle of the London Eye
was stark against the skyline, moonbeams picking out
the glass capsules. Further away, she could just make
out the beautiful, architectural form of the Houses of
Parliament.

Ben moved closer to her, and they stood there for a
while, her head resting against his, their bodies touching, and Jade was content, more so than she'd been in
a long, long time.

'Aren't you two coming back on to the dance floor?'
Jack was clearly in a mischievous mood. 'You can't stay
like that for ever, you know. Matt's going to do a solo
number. You can't miss it.'

'Of course we can't.' Ben looked at Jade, giving her a
wry smile, and they made their way back into the midst
of the throng.

He was good company, he made her laugh, and they
danced and chatted for the next hour or so, joining the
rest of the gang on the dance floor or at the tables.

Matt joined them for a few minutes while he took a
break. 'I've been practising some new numbers for the
past few weeks,' Matt was saying. 'I think they turned
out pretty well in the end. It felt good, playing to this
crowd, anyway.'

'It's been a great night,' Jade told him. 'I'm certain
everyone here has loved the music.'

'She's right,' Ben said. 'Are you quite sure you're
studying for the right profession? I imagine you could
earn a good living if you stayed with the band.'

Matt laughed. 'Maybe. But I want to be a doctor. For me, music is just a release from all the pressure.'

He stood up and emptied his glass, then went to join the rest of the band members on stage, preparing for the last session of the evening. Ben led Jade on to the dance floor once more, and they lost themselves in the music for a while.

When the band played a slow number, they clung together, cheek to cheek, and Jade loved the closeness, the way they moved together as one. If she could only keep herself from getting too deeply involved with him, she might still be safe.

'I've really enjoyed being with you tonight,' she said softly, looking up into his eyes as the music faded away.

'Me, too. I was hoping you would see what it's like to get out and enjoy life for a change. We should do it again.'

She nodded, but her eyes clouded a fraction. 'Just as long as it's clear there are no strings. I'm sorry, but I'm still not ready for anything more than this.'

He gently ran the back of his hand down over her cheek. 'At least it's a start,' he said.

CHAPTER SIX

'So, is that settled then…? Are we all meeting up by the wharf this afternoon?' Matt helped himself to more rashers of crisp bacon from the pan, and carefully slid them between two rounds of toast.

'Um…I'll be working at the café bar until mid-afternoon,' Jade said. 'I'd like to have left earlier but that's the best I can manage. I'll come and find you as soon as I've finished there, if you're planning on staying around the wharf area.' She dipped bread into the yolk of her fried egg and looked up at him.

Matt nodded. 'We only planned on moving as far as the market, last time we talked about it. There should be plenty of people milling about, wanting to hand over cash for good causes.' He looked at the charity tins assembled on the kitchen worktop. 'All being well, we should raise a lot of money.'

Jade glanced at Ben and Lucy, seated at the other end of the table. 'I'll be able to stay and help out for two or three hours at least, but then I have to go and meet up with my father.' She sobered at the thought, and Ben must have caught her sombre expression, because his eyes narrowed as he studied her thoughtfully.

'Does that bother you...going to see your father?'

She was hesitant. 'I'm not sure. A bit.' Even now, she found it difficult to talk to her father. She'd been ten years old when he'd left, and a lot of years had passed since then, but she still couldn't quite forgive him for walking out on his family. Something major had gone wrong with the father-daughter relationship...a lack of trust, perhaps, on her part.

'It's bound to be difficult to make a real bond, when he's missed a good chunk of your growing up. But I imagine he must be proud of you, now that you're studying medicine.'

'I suppose so.'

'It's good that you go on meeting, though. If you keep doing that, with any luck, things should work themselves out, eventually.' He looked her over once more, giving her an assessing kind of glance, and then he shook his head. 'I don't know how you go on doing as much as you do and still manage to stay serene—going out to work and putting in shifts at the hospital, I mean. Perhaps this afternoon will turn out to be a pleasant change for you.'

She smiled. 'Yes, I expect so.'

'I'll have to leave around two o'clock,' Lucy murmured, pouring coffee. 'So I'll only be able to manage about an hour's collecting, I'm afraid.' She looked a little pale, her long, golden hair lending her an ethereal quality just then. Her blue eyes were troubled, making Jade wonder if something was wrong, but then Lucy added, 'I have to go home for the weekend—well, I'll be away at least until Monday evening, I think. I'll miss a couple of lectures, but I can easily get hold of what I need online to catch up. Something's come up at home, and my parents have asked me to visit.'

'Is someone ill?' Jade asked, immediately concerned for her.

'No, it's more of a business thing, as far as I know. I just hope it's nothing that affects this house—but your tenancies are all secure for the next few months,' she added hurriedly, 'so there's nothing for any of you to worry about, whatever happens.' She glanced at Matt. 'Has your father said anything to you about what might be going on?'

Matt shook his head. His father was a business partner of Martyn Clements, Lucy's father, so it would have been quite natural if he'd heard something. He frowned. 'I'll give him a ring later today.'

'Okay.' Lucy glanced at Jade. 'Do you think you could pick up my computer from the repair shop on your way to work? The place closes at twelve on a Saturday, so you'd be doing me a great favour. That way, I'll have it for Monday evening, and I'll be able to do some catching up on any study topics I've missed at the hospital.'

'Yes, of course.'

Lucy handed her the repair ticket, and Jade put it away securely in her bag.

'That's me done,' Jade said, pushing her plate to one side and swallowing the last of her coffee. 'I must go. Sorry to rush off.' She looked at the men. 'It's your turn to do the washing-up, remember?'

Matt put on a pained expression. 'Did I mention this

horrible rash I get whenever my hands go anywhere near soap suds?' he asked.

Lucy gave him a sweet smile. 'Poor you.' She reached for his hands and inspected them. 'Hmm. Not a blemish as yet. Very fortunate, that, and the good news is, we have several pairs of rubber gloves for you to choose from, so you'll be able to keep them that way.' She got to her feet and picked up her coffee mug. 'I'm off upstairs to pack an overnight bag.'

Ben grinned at Matt. 'Well, at least it was worth a try.' Matt pulled a face, his shoulders hunched in resignation.

Jade picked up one of the charity tins and went off to her waitressing job. She did as Lucy asked, picking up the iPad on her way, and then slid it into a discreet interior pocket in her bag.

'Would it be all right with you if I leave the collecting tin on the counter?' she asked Jacques when she arrived at the café bar. 'You never know. People might feel inclined to empty their spare cash in there.'

He nodded. '*Oui*. Go ahead. As long as you don't wave it under people's noses, that will be fine.'

As the day went on, she noticed more and more people stopping to drop coins into the slot, so that by the time her shift ended, the tin was reasonably heavy, and she smiled inwardly. It was a good start. All the money would go to research to help sick children.

She walked to the door and was startled to see Ben waiting there for her. 'I thought I'd come and meet you, rather than have you wander round on your own, looking for us,' he explained. 'Lucy's already on her way home to Berkshire.'

'That was thoughtful of you.' She looked into his eyes, her mouth curving. It was great that he'd taken the trouble to do that. 'Thanks.'

'You're welcome.' His answering smile made her feel warm and cosseted and, as they stepped out into the sunlit afternoon, she glanced at him obliquely. He was completely at ease, his features relaxed, and the thought crossed her mind that she was more than happy to be walking along with him as if she didn't have a care in the world.

For these few moments, at least, it was as though they were perfectly in tune with one another. In a lot of ways it would be good to get together with Ben, to be a couple and share a special relationship—it was just that for her, relationships had a way of ending badly.

'We'll go to the wharf and start shaking our tins around there, if you like,' he said. 'This will be my second time around. Matt and I have already swapped full tins for empties and given them to Lucy to take back to the house.'

She nodded. 'Brilliant. I've a feeling this is going to be a great day. We're going to do really well.'

The corners of his eyes crinkled in response to her smile. 'I think so, too. It's even better now that you're here.' Then he brought his thoughts back to the task in hand. 'Mind you, there are a lot of students out and about, all with collecting tins for various causes. They're not all from the medical school.'

The wharf was just a short distance away, and it was

only a minute or so before they came across the life-size replica of the *Golden Hinde*, the sixteenth-century galleon that Sir Francis Drake used to sail around the world.

'They're having a pirates' day for the children,' Ben told her with a smile, 'so it's all "What ho, me hearties," and old sea shanties.'

The children were having a great time, from what Jade could see. They were climbing on the huge cannon and looking through spy-glasses, and generally whooping it up, while their parents wandered in desultory fashion in front of the ship, eating ice creams and soaking up the sun. There were ship's officers in sixteenth-century costume along with ordinary seamen, ready to do battle with the marauding, evil-looking pirates. The pirates wore bandanas and billowing shirts along with dark breeches.

Ben disappeared into the crowd a minute or two after they arrived, murmuring an excuse and leaving her with Matt. Jade frowned momentarily, wondering where he had gone, but then she dismissed it from her mind. He wouldn't be far away. He wouldn't simply leave her. She went with Matt among the crowd, shaking her tin.

'They're certainly in a generous mood,' she said a while later, and Matt nodded.

Then Ben reappeared and she stared at him in startled disbelief. He must have been to one of the stalls nearby, because he was wearing a colourful bandana and black eye patch, and sporting a lethal-looking cutlass. Somehow he looked incredibly sexy, like one of those vigorous, roguish men from yesteryear, and her heart gave an involuntary leap in her chest.

A moment later, he slid his arm around her waist, gripping her firmly like a prize and catching her totally unawares. 'That's better. I have you to myself at last,' he said, his voice deep and dark. 'This is my lucky day.'

Jade had a feeling it was hers, too. She laughed at him, loving the way his strong arm wrapped around her, pulling her against his hard chest. She could feel the steady thud of his heartbeat. His head was close to hers, and she felt the warmth of his skin against her cheek. Children watched them wide-eyed, and he held on to her, his eyes gleaming with amusement. 'She's mine,' he told them all with a wicked leer, beginning to edge her away from the mass of people. 'All mine, and there's nothing you can do to stop me.'

'Help, help,' she cried, trying not to laugh. 'Help me.'

A cluster of boys crowded around, joining in the fun. 'Give her up, mister, or else...' They aimed their weapons at him menacingly.

He tightened his grip on her. 'Never. Not even if you put money in the tin,' he scoffed. Then, 'Well, maybe, possibly...' He rattled the container at the parents. Some of them obliged cheerfully and he put on a sinful smile. 'Hah! Fooled you,' he said with a fiendish laugh. 'Did you really think I'd give up my treasure? Me? Think again. I'm a pirate! I'll have my wicked way with her and none can stop me.'

With that, he turned her in his arms and proceeded to kiss her soundly, while the children squealed with delight. Jade, when she could gather together any thoughts at all under the sudden onslaught, found herself mar-velling, *Wow, if this is pretence, he's making a darned good job of it.* She was completely bowled over by him, his mouth coming down fiercely on hers, his hand flat-tening against her waist and drawing her ever closer to him. The kiss was passionate, fast and thorough, and well worthy of any pirate. Sensation after sensation rocketed through her, the blood roared in her head, and her heart was booming so heavily she was sure every-one must be able to hear it.

Then all at once, everything changed. The kiss ended, and Ben, one hand still around her waist, was fighting off children with swords and daggers, until he laughingly said, 'Okay, okay, I surrender.' He winked at Jade. 'Got my six pennyworth, anyway.'

She was breathless, still speechless and dazed with the sheer exuberance of that wonderful, tempestuous kiss. She didn't know whether to laugh out loud or mourn the loss of his warm, strong body next to hers. All she knew was that the heat of those pillaging lips had left an imprint that would burn for ever in her mind.

The excited children weren't about to give up. Ben sheathed his cutlass through a belt loop and said, 'Shiver me timbers, you'll all be the death o' me, so you will.' He pretended to be wounded, and finally, reluctantly cast her off.

The children cheered and after a while, when the excitement died down, they gradually drifted away to find further adventures.

Matt was chuckling, going around the crowd, hold-ing out his tin to all and sundry, and all the while Jade tried to recover herself, watching Ben with a bemused expression.

'You look all pink-cheeked and flustered,' he said, his dark eyes gleaming. 'I didn't shock you too much, did I?'

'I wouldn't say shocked, exactly,' she said with a rueful smile. 'I think I'm more stunned than anything.'

He bent his head close to hers. 'I don't regret it,' he murmured, 'not for an instant. In fact, I've been wanting to do that for an awful long time.'

Jade looked at him, her eyes widening. 'You *are* a pirate,' she said, 'through and through.' Inside her, a little glimmer of heat started up. It could easily be fanned into flame, and her stomach quivered nervously at the thought.

'Maybe I am, where you're concerned,' he murmured.

Matt came to join them, unwittingly breaking up the intimate moment. 'Shall we move on?' he suggested.

They went on from there to a seventeenth-century coaching inn, a marvellous, galleried building, where people were sitting at tables set out on the cobbled forecourt. They went around collecting for a while, but then, with the heat of the sun beating down on them, they were all becoming thirsty.

'Let's go and get a drink,' Ben suggested, and the other two readily agreed.

Inside the inn, Jade glanced around, impressed by the ancient oak beams and latticed windows. It was like being a small part of history.

Ben removed his eye-patch. 'What will you have?'

'Something long and cool,' Jade answered. 'Fruit juice with ice would be lovely.'

'Okay.'

Matt went with him to the bar, leaving Jade to look around. The doors had been left open to let in the afternoon sunshine, and there was a cheerful, relaxed atmosphere everywhere.

'Shall we find a table outside?' Ben led the way, and even though it was crowded, they managed to find somewhere to sit when another group of people stood up to go.

There was a covered food market close by, with stalls spilling out onto the street, and Jade could hear the stall-holders calling out to the customers. Wonderful smells wafted over the air to her, strong cheeses and freshly baked bread that made her mouth water.

'Are you hungry?' Ben asked, watching her sniff the air. 'They do excellent sandwiches here, with really tasty chips. I could get some for all of us.'

'I'd love that, thanks.'

Matt nodded. 'Me, too. You stay here,' he said to Ben. 'I'll go and order them.'

He went over to the bar to order the food.

'That market was around in Charles Dickens' time,' Ben said, following her gaze. 'They say he often used to come here to drink the ale.'

'Did he?' She paused for a moment to absorb the history of the place. 'I wonder if he did any writing while he was here?' She paused to take it all in...the people, the sounds, the smells, the general air of happiness. She could imagine the writer sitting at one of the tables, thinking out his stories.

'Maybe. He mentioned the place in one of his books...*Little Dorrit*, I think.' Ben swallowed his cold beer, closing his eyes to relish the moment.

They stayed at the inn for an hour or so, before Matt pointed out that it was probably time to make a move. 'We could do a bit more collecting, if you like, but then I need to start heading for home so that I can make that call to my father.' He looked at his watch and then glanced at Ben. 'Didn't you say you had to be on duty at the hospital some time soon?'

Ben winced. 'Unfortunately, yes, I'm on the late shift.' He looked at Jade through his lashes. 'Though I'd far sooner stay here for another hour or two.' His dark eyes glittered with hidden meaning.

Jade lowered her head a fraction and smiled under his provocative gaze. 'So would I. It's been a fun afternoon and I'd love it if it were to last a little longer. But like I said this morning, my father's coming into the City today, and we've arranged to meet up at a coffee shop. I'll stay on in the city and wander around the shops for half an hour before I have to go and meet him.'

They stood up to leave, and Ben put an arm around her shoulders. 'It's been good to see you looking happy and relaxed,' he murmured.

She leaned into his embrace. She'd had a taste of fun and excitement, and inside she was fizzing, wanting more. Could things work out for them? Was she wrong to be so cautious?

On her own, some time later, she wandered around

the streets, looking in shop windows and stopping every now and again to make a small purchase.

As Ben had said earlier, there had been plenty of students around, enjoying a day out in the city, and they were here still, so there was noise and laughter even after the main crowds had drifted away. Glancing at her watch, she decided it was time to go and meet her father. Maybe, after that, she would go home and run a bath and soak for half an hour or so and maybe take the rest of the evening off for once. She'd had a taste of freedom, freedom from pressure, from the constant need to study and from the worry of needing to earn her keep. She made a rueful smile. It was all Ben's fault—he'd goaded her into letting go, and she had discovered that she loved every minute of it.

Her phone beeped and she stopped to rummage in her bag and retrieve the text message. 'Hi, Jade,' she read. 'I'll be arriving in London in a few hours. Maybe we could meet up soon? I really need to talk to you. I've had a long time to think things through. I love you. Ewan.'

Jade clutched a hand to her chest as the breath left her body. Ewan was coming home? He loved her? What was going on? How could this be happening, now, after all this time? How long had it been? A year?

She didn't know what to think, how to respond.

'Where you goin', sweetheart? You comin' my way?' She came to a sudden halt as a young man appeared in front of her, barring her way.

'Sorry, not today,' she muttered. She didn't want to have to deal with anyone right now. This youth was in his late teens, she guessed, and he'd obviously been drinking because she could smell it on his breath.

'Aw, don't be like that.' A friend came from behind her to join him, and that worried her a little because she felt trapped. When she tried to sidestep him, he followed her movements. 'Pretty girl like you shouldn't be on your own.'

She started to be afraid then. There was no one else around just now, but maybe, if she needed to, she could shout out and someone would come from one of the side streets. With any luck, though, it wouldn't come to that.

'I really need to get home,' she said. 'Please let me pass.'

'Please let me pass…pretty please,' the first one mimicked, making a grab for her. She batted his hands away.

The other one began to tug at her bag. 'What's in here, then? The Crown Jewels? You been up to the Tower?' He snatched it from her, and a ripple of anger shot through her like wildfire.

'That's enough from the pair of you,' she said, her voice sharp. 'Stop messing about and give it back.'

'Nah. Don't think I will.' He peeled back the zip, rummaging about in there.

She started to press buttons on the keypad of her phone. 'Okay, I'm going to call the police. You'd better stop what you're doing and be on your way.' In the next instant the other youth tugged the phone from her hands and tossed it over a high wall.

'Try phoning now.' He laughed.

'Yeah.' The first youth flung her bag after the phone,

and she stared in frustration as her belongings disappeared, one by one, out of sight. Inside she was screaming, No...no... How could they do that? How could this be happening? How could this whole day disintegrate in just a few minutes?

There was absolutely nothing she could have done to prevent it, and all the pent-up feelings inside her boiled over. 'How dare you?' she raged. 'You'll not get away with this.' They laughed at her and ran off down the street, vanishing into an alleyway and leaving her to stare after them in abject frustration. Of course they would get away with it.

She looked back at the wall. How on earth was she going to retrieve her bag and the phone? It was too high for her to climb, and the top was covered in dangerous-looking spikes. Looking around, she discovered that the building was an empty office block, with a 'To Let' sign fixed to the side wall. By peering through some railings close by, she saw that the wall enclosed a patch of waste ground. There was a door to the main building, but it was locked, and further along there was a padlocked gate set into the wall.

For some minutes she simply stood in the street as despair washed over her. She had no idea what to do. If only Ben had been here, she was sure this wouldn't have happened.

She memorised the name of the letting agents, resolving to ring them later. And then as she gathered her breath and took stock of everything that had happened, she felt a tide of dismay wash over her. What was she going to do about Ewan? She ought to get in touch with him at some point, and it was probably important for her to meet up with him, if only to work out how she truly felt. Was there a chance she could put all this angst behind her?

But for now time was moving on, and she still had to go and see her father. He would be waiting for her.

He was pleased to see her, and if he noticed that she was a little distracted, he said nothing. She didn't tell him what had happened, but listened to his tale of moving house. He wanted to know how her mother was getting along with her new husband, and he sounded wistful when he spoke of her. Had he learned, too late, that the grass wasn't always greener on the other side?

That meeting was still on her mind the next day, but Ewan's message and the loss of her bag pervaded everything. Lucy's computer was in there, and she would be devastated to have lost it. A good deal of her work was stored in there.

There was no one she could confide in. Ben didn't come in from work until the morning, and then he went up to his room to sleep for a while. Matt was out, and Jade felt the problem weighing her down. After work at the café bar, she tried to study, but it was no use. Her mind just couldn't take anything in.

So she called Ewan from the house phone and left a message on his voice mail to say that she would meet him the following weekend, before she went to work at the café bar.

After that, her biggest worry was how to explain things to Ben. How would he react when he discovered she was going to see Ewan?

CHAPTER SEVEN

On Monday morning, she went into work with a feeling of lead in her chest. Professor Farnham was expecting her to present a case to him today as part of her ongoing assessment, and that was going to be something of an ordeal because, try as she might, she couldn't think clearly.

'We have a four-year-old boy with hip pain in the observation ward,' Mandy told her when she arrived in Paediatrics. The nurse moved away from the nurses' station where she had been standing with Ben. He was looking through paperwork, but he glanced up as Jade came towards the desk.

'Professor Farnham said you would be doing the boy's case history and examination this morning,' he commented.

'That's right, yes.' She wanted to talk to him, to tell him what was on her mind, but this wasn't the time. The trouble was, she had no idea when she might find the right moment.

He came over to her and handed her the child's file. 'Take your time,' he murmured, clasping her hand for a second or two. 'Just remember to do a thorough examination and order any relevant tests. You'll be fine.'

Jade gave a weak smile, but she wasn't so sure about that. With Professor Farnham standing over her a few minutes later, her brain turned to cotton wool. Ben was there, too. As a foundation-year doctor, he was expected to sanction tests and organise treatment. In a way, he was being tested, too.

On the observation ward, the little boy was thoroughly miserable. He was tired and in pain, and his face was streaked with tears. Jade wanted to pick him up and cuddle him.

'He hasn't had much sleep lately,' his mother said. 'The pain keeps him awake at night. I don't know what to do. I'm at my wits' end.'

'That's understandable,' Jade murmured. She thought they both looked tired, mother and son.

'Do you think you could stand up for me, Tim—just for a minute?' Jade asked. She wanted to see how the boy walked, but his face reddened and he started to cry.

'No,' he sobbed. 'Don't want to stand up.'

'Um…that…that's okay,' Jade said hurriedly. That wasn't a very good start, was it? Flustered, she began again. 'It must be very painful for you.' Instead of appeasing him, her words provoked more loud sobs.

Jade bit her lip. 'Perhaps, if you lie there, I could just take a look at your leg?' she said.

'No.' His eyes blazed with determination. 'Don't you look at my leg.' He was shouting at her through his tears, shaking his head vigorously. 'No one's touching my leg.' His face crumpled. 'Just make the pain go 'way.'

'Yes, of course, we'll do that for you, Tim.' She tried to reassure him. 'I'm just trying to find out what's wrong with your leg so that we can give you the right medicine. Just you lie back and rest for a bit.' This was awful. She felt the heat rising in her cheeks. Nothing was going right for her. She went to lay the case file down on the bed, but the boy moved at the same time and the file hit the floor, sending papers everywhere. To one side of her, she heard the professor's deep sigh.

Ben knelt down to help her pick up the papers. 'Calm down,' he whispered. 'Take a deep breath. You can do this.'

She gave an almost imperceptible nod. Getting to her feet, she pulled up a chair and sat down opposite the mother. She dragged air into her lungs and began again, asking her about the boy's symptoms. 'I see from the triage notes that this pain came on suddenly. Has he had an infection of some sort recently?'

The mother shook her head. 'There's been nothing like that.'

'What about a recent fall? I know it says here in the notes that he hasn't fallen, but can you think back? Has there been anything at all in the last few weeks?'

The woman frowned. 'Well, he came off a swing at the park about three weeks ago, but he didn't seem too badly hurt at the time, and it's only this last week that he's started to limp.'

'I see.' Jade studied the X-ray film. 'From the looks of things, there's some inflammation around the hip joint, but nothing's broken, which is good.' She frowned, trying to work out the best course of action. 'I think we'll need to do some blood tests to find out if there's any infection going on in there, and in the meantime we'll start him on some anti-inflammatory medication. That will ease the pain, and then later, all being well, we can apply heat and massage to relieve the symptoms.'

'So what's wrong with him?' his mother asked. 'If you're looking for infection, it's not come about from a simple fall, has it?'

'We have to do the tests purely to rule out other things,' Jade said. 'I believe Tim has a condition called transient synovitis. The membrane around the joint becomes inflamed, but with a period of rest it should settle down. I think we should admit him, though, so that we can observe things and make sure that he stays off the leg. We may decide that traction would help—we would put straps around the leg to lift it a little and take the strain off the hip.' She smiled. 'It can be difficult to keep a young child in that position for long, but we'll see how it goes.'

Her confidence building once more, she turned back to Tim. He was covering his face with his arm. 'Now, then, young Tim,' she murmured, 'I think I may have someone here that you'd like to meet. Just give me a minute.'

She could see his interest was pricked. He was looking at her with curiosity, his eyes almost shielded by his arm. She stood up and went over to a filing cabinet on the other side of the room. Coming back towards the bed, she held up a teddy bear. 'This is Toby Bear,' she told him, adding, 'Look, he has a poorly leg, just like you.' She pointed to the bandage around the bear's leg. 'But we can give him some medicine to help the pain go away, and then, when he's feeling a bit better, we can look at the bit that hurts and see if we can make him well again.' She gave him the bear. 'Would you like to hold him?'

He nodded, still looking at her from behind his elbow, but then he reached for the cuddly toy and felt the silky fur against his cheek. After a moment or two he wrapped his arms around the bear, holding him close to his chest. He lay back against the pillows and closed his eyes.

Jade watched him for a moment and then smiled, turning back to his mother. 'I'll just go and talk to my colleagues for a while, and then we'll organise his medication,' she said. 'Excuse me, please.'

She stood up and went with Professor Farnham and Ben to the other side of the room.

'Hmm.' The professor was preoccupied for a moment or two, and Jade's heart sank. Had she completely and utterly failed? She should have done the examination after all.

Ben's grey-blue gaze meshed with hers. It was as though he was sending out encouraging messages of comfort and support, but nothing would cheer her right now.

Professor Farnham looked at her. 'Awkward situation, that, when a toddler doesn't want to be examined, but you handled it just fine. Well done. Good diagnosis.

But you need to do the examination when you get the chance.' He smiled at both of them. 'Carry on.'

He left the room and Jade breathed a sigh of relief. Ben gave her a thumbs-up sign and would have stayed to talk to her, except that Tim's mother caught his attention. He went to speak to her and answer her questions.

Distracted still, Jade wrote up the prescription for the child's medication and went to find Mandy to organise it.

'What happened back there?' Ben asked, coming to join her a few minutes later. 'I know it was awkward, with the toddler crying and all, and you handled it fine, but I had the feeling something was wrong right from the beginning. You didn't seem as though you were your usual self. You seemed subdued.'

'I was nervous, I suppose.'

He shook his head. 'I wondered about that, but you've always managed really well before this. You worry, but you're keen to learn and you pretty much always know what you're doing. I think there's something else. Did it upset you, meeting with your father the other evening?'

She winced. 'Not really,' she murmured. 'I mean, it was a bit awkward, because he wanted to know all about my mother…how things were going with her and my stepfather. He seemed to have some vague regrets about leaving her—or maybe his pride was piqued because she found someone to replace him, someone she could love. It took her a long while to get over my father, and I'm sorry to say it but I think he quite enjoyed that at the time. In a sick way, it boosted his ego.'

Ben sucked in his breath. 'I think it's pretty clear why you have problems with men. It's all about commitment, isn't it? Between them, your father and Ewan have done a good job on you.'

She didn't answer him. Recklessly, yesterday, she'd thought she might risk getting involved, throwing caution to the wind, but not any more. The fever of delirium had waned and now she was seeing things in the clear light of day. Relationships were messy things and people could get hurt.

He said cautiously, 'But if it wasn't your father who upset you, what was it? I know there's something on your mind. I could see it in your face when you came on to the ward.'

She hesitated. 'You aren't going to like it.'

He frowned. 'Tell me. Whatever it is, I'm sure I can handle it. We need to be open with one another if we're going to get anywhere at all.'

She closed her eyes briefly. 'I had a text message from Ewan the other day. He's back in London, and he wants to meet up with me.' There, she'd said it...it was out in the open. She looked at him, anxious to see what his reaction would be.

His eyes widened. Then he pulled in a deep breath and said, 'Have you spoken to him? What are you going to do?'

'I think—I think I should go and see him.'

His brows met in a dark line and she hurried to say, 'I've been unhappy for a long time, in a kind of void, unable to move on, and I can't see any way out. I was upset when we parted company, but it isn't that...I'm over that. It's just that I feel as though I'm in limbo and I don't know if I can ever trust anyone again. I need to sort things out, once and for all, and perhaps if I meet up with him I'll be able to think more clearly. I left a message on his voice mail saying I would meet him for coffee at the weekend.'

He didn't say anything for a while. Then he said in a terse voice, 'So I guess you must have been keeping in touch ever since you split up? He didn't seem to have any trouble contacting you, or you him.'

'That's only natural, isn't it? We were together for quite a while.'

His eyes narrowed. 'How do you feel about him? You say you're over it, but you've been distracted this last day or so, and I can't help thinking that's down to him.'

'I'm not sure about that. To be honest, I feel a bit numb, as though I'm in a bit of a daze.' She frowned. 'Mind you, that might be because I…' She broke off. How could she tell him that she'd been foolish enough to lose Lucy's computer? It would cost her several weeks' wages to replace it, but even then she couldn't do anything about the lost data. And now was hardly the time to mention it, when she'd just stunned him with her news.

'Because you what?'

'Nothing. It doesn't matter.'

His breath left his lips in an angry hiss. 'Just tell me. Get it over with. It can't be any worse than what you've just told me. Can it?'

She shook her head. 'I ran into a problem yesterday,

after you and Matt left.' Quickly, she told him what had happened. 'I'm really worried about Lucy's computer. I have to get it back. I rang the lettings agency, but they say there's nothing they can do.' Her shoulders drooped. 'I'm completely out of answers.'

'We'll go over there after work and I'll take a look.'

She turned her startled gaze on him. 'You mean you'll come with me?'

He nodded.

'I never thought... Thanks, Ben. I was beginning to despair.' She gave a small sigh of relief. She didn't know what good it would do, but he had offered to help and that gave her hope. It comforted her to know that he would do that for her even though she had disappointed him.

All day long she fretted about the business with Ewan and the way Ben had responded. Added to that, she was worried about getting her belongings back. But she forced herself to concentrate on her work, and by the end of her shift she had managed to examine the little boy and confirm her diagnosis. His blood tests showed no sign of sepsis, and that was a great relief all round.

She checked up on her other patients. Jason had recovered from his diabetic crisis and was almost ready to be discharged. Owen, the child with a rash caused by inflammation of his blood vessels, was getting better little by little. At least some things were looking up.

'Okay, show me where this incident happened,' Ben said, meeting up with her after work ended. They left the hospital together but his mood was uncertain and she was quiet as they approached the office building a short time later.

'The boys threw my phone and handbag over the wall, here,' she told him. 'It's so high, I don't see any way of getting over it. There are some railings further on but again they're too high and with spikes on top. There's a main door, and a gate around the side, but everything's locked up.'

He walked with her around the outside of the building until they reached the gate, made of sturdy hardwood and set into the brick wall. 'You're right—you mentioned it was padlocked this afternoon, but I'll see what I can do.' He reached into his pocket and pulled out a couple of paperclips. 'I thought I might need these,' he said, seeing her quizzical look. He glanced about him to make sure no one was around.

Then he bent the clips into L shapes and inserted first one, then the other, into the lock. He twisted and tugged, and within a few seconds there was a satisfying click as the lock popped. 'We're in,' he said, pocketing the paper clips. 'You stay there,' he added, when she would have gone with him. 'There's no point in both of us risking getting into trouble.'

She decided it might be best if she acted as a lookout. He was in there for several minutes, long enough for her to begin to fret. No one came by, but she was more than thankful when he finally reappeared.

'Got them,' he said, his expression triumphant. 'The bag was hidden in some long grass, so it took me a while to find it.' He handed the bag and phone to her and then turned to make sure the padlock was secure once more.

She put the phone inside her bag and let out a slow breath. 'Thank you, Ben,' she said, her voice breaking a little with emotion. 'You don't know how relieved I am to have them back. I'm just so glad that you found them for me.' She looked up at him, wanting to hold him, and show him how grateful she was. Without realising it, she had laid a hand on his arm, her face upturned to his, and that was all it took for the dam to break.

His arms went round her, his head lowered, and the next thing she knew, he was kissing her tenderly, his lips tasting hers as if they were vintage wine, something to be experienced slowly, lovingly, with complete reverence. She responded as a desert flower responded to water. Her whole body came alive with that kiss. She curled her hand around the nape of his neck, loving the feel of him, the way his hard body became one with her softly feminine form, the way his hands gently caressed her and shaped her curves.

'I need you, Jade,' he murmured raggedly after a while, stopping to draw breath. 'I want you. I know you said "no strings", but I can't settle for that. I care about you and I don't want to think of you with anyone else, especially not Ewan.'

His thigh moved against hers, and she felt desire unfurl inside her like a pool of molten lava. It flowed through every pore of her being, leaving her feeling feverish, wanting something more, something indefinable but infinitely pleasurable.

'I'm not with anyone else,' she whispered.

'Maybe not at this moment,' he said. 'It was supposed to be over between you two, and yet you're going to see him again. I think the trouble is you don't know your own mind.'

'You don't understand,' she said huskily.

'No, I don't.' Just then sounds drifted towards them, snatches of conversation, footsteps tapping along the pavement. He sighed and slowly released her. 'I'd forgotten we were in the street,' he said flatly. 'Maybe we should get away from here before anybody comes and finds us.'

'Yes.' She nodded, reluctantly accepting the loss of his warm body next to hers, sad because those hands were no longer seeking out every curve and hollow. She'd learned something in these last few minutes. She wanted him, more than she'd ever wanted any man. He'd cast a spell on her, she was bewitched, and she was sure she would never be the same again.

They walked along the street, heading for home. 'All being well, your phone should still work okay,' he said. His tone was matter-of-fact, and he seemed to have put their close interlude behind him. 'It had fallen in quite a sheltered spot, so it should have stayed dry.'

She nodded, but didn't say anything. She was still overwhelmed by what had happened between them.

'I don't know about the computer,' he said with a frown. 'It ought to have been all right inside the bag but it's only a canvas covering, so I can't be sure.'

'It'll be fine,' she answered, finding her voice. 'It was wrapped in a safety envelope in an inside pocket.'

'Good. That's a relief—Lucy will be pleased.'

'Yes.' She sent him a sideways glance. 'I still can't get over how easily you did it. How did you come to know about picking a lock? That's a bit out of the normal run of things, isn't it?'

He gave a wry smile. 'I suppose I had what you might call a misspent youth.'

She raised her brows. 'Really? So you weren't kidding when you said you might have given everyone a few grey hairs?' She studied him, suddenly intrigued.

He shook his head. 'I got into all kinds of trouble when I was a teenager. All the usual stuff that boys do, I suppose—unruly boys,' he added. 'It wasn't too bad, really, to begin with….things like using makeshift rafts on lakes, being where I shouldn't be, climbing on roofs or over fences, scrumping fruit from orchards—for no reason other than I could.'

'Were you the unruly influence, or your friends?' They walked by the market and passed alongside the galleon, all quiet now.

He frowned. 'The thing was, when I was twelve or thirteen, one of my friends went down with flu and became very ill, very quickly. It turned to pneumonia and he almost died. I think it taught us both that life can be very fragile…fleeting, even. And when he was fully recovered he'd changed in some ways. He wanted to get whatever he could out of life. He developed a bit of a wild side—well, we both did. He showed me how to pick locks and get into places where we shouldn't have been—broken-down sheds and empty buildings and so on.'

She let out a slow breath. 'I can't imagine your parents, or his, being happy about any of that.'

He winced. 'You're right, it was probably a difficult

time for them, though we didn't do anything worse—
at least, we fell just short of it, I think. It was all a big
adventure for us. We were warned off a few times by
irate adults and we ended up being grounded by our
parents more often than not.'

'So what happened to bring you back on to the
straight and narrow?'

'My grandfather. He was a great man. He never con-
demned, but he was always ready to listen. And talking
helped. And then of course, that day when my friend's
sister collapsed I finally realised that I'd been behav-
ing stupidly. There was so much more to be had from
life, and I needed to get my act together.'

'Was that when you decided to take up medicine?'

'Not exactly. I think the idea must have planted itself
in my head back then, but I was still very young and
unsure of myself. It took a few years before I properly
made up my mind.'

They had almost reached home by now. The leafy
avenue came into view, and Jade's thoughts became
sombre. Ben had lapsed into silence, and she wondered
if he was thinking about her and Ewan.

She ought to have been able to convince him that he
didn't matter to them, but right now it seemed like an
insurmountable object in their path, and perhaps that
was because she didn't know herself how things would
go when she met him once again.

CHAPTER EIGHT

'SOMETHING smells good.' Lucy came into the kitchen around lunchtime and sniffed the air. 'Mmm…really good. It's making me hungry.' She smiled at Jade. 'What are you making?'

'Chocolate fudge cake.' Jade was spreading the fudge filling on two upturned halves of the cake. 'I thought I'd take advantage of lectures being cancelled for the morning and get on with it. It's for Ben, actually, to thank him for helping me out yesterday. I wanted to do it sooner, but this is the first chance I've had.'

'You mean it's a thank-you for finding your bag and phone? And my computer?'

'That's right. I seem to remember him saying this was his favourite. I thought I'd give it to him when we sit down to eat this evening.'

Lucy was pensive for a moment. 'Maybe I'm the one who ought to be baking for him. I don't know how I'd have gone on without my computer—all my notes are on there.' She shook her head. 'Still, all's well that ends well, as they say.'

'That's true. And at least your weekend at home

wasn't as worrying as you thought it might be—more of a family meeting you said, didn't you?'

Lucy nodded. 'Dad's thinking about expanding the business, and he wanted to talk about a new allocation of shares and so on.' She frowned. 'It means Matt's father will be taking on more work, though, and I don't think he's too pleased about that. Which, in turn, means Matt's not going to be very happy with me and my family.'

'It's an awkward situation for you.'

'Yes, it is.' Lucy glanced at the two sponge halves, upturned on wire trays, and perked up a bit. 'I know Ben will just love that cake. But why don't you take it in to him at work this afternoon, instead of waiting till this evening? Anyway, if you bring it out at supper, Matt will scoff most of it. You know what he's like if there are any goodies around.'

'You're right.' Jade laughed. 'I suppose I *could* take it in to the hospital this afternoon. Ben's been having a rough time of it this week because one of his patients is a young girl with food poisoning that has affected her kidneys. She's been going downhill fast. You never know, this might help to brighten his day just a little.'

For herself, she hadn't come properly down to earth since he'd kissed her the other afternoon, and now she was in a quandary about how to go on where Ben was concerned. All she could think about was being with him, but this business with Ewan had set them back, clouding the issue, and Ben had been subdued of late.

At work, of course, her feelings had to take second place. It was essential that she concentrate on the job in hand, and everything she did, every new task, every procedure she undertook, had to be noted down in her electronic profile as part of her ongoing assessment. She couldn't afford to let things slide, even if she was overcome by new and unsettling emotions. The problem was, she'd never felt this way before and she didn't quite know how to handle the situation.

This afternoon, though, her first port of call was to go and check up on four-year-old Tim, who had been in such pain at the beginning of the week. She wanted to make sure the medication and enforced rest were working. When she'd examined him last, his hip had been warm and tender to the touch.

'How are you doing, young man?' she asked him, going over to his bed and checking his chart. Everything seemed to be progressing smoothly, and the little boy's leg was being supported at a forty-five degree angle, in order to take the strain off his hip.

He lifted his shoulders. 'Okay.' He was lying back against his pillows, concentrating on colouring in a page in a picture book.

'Okay? Does that mean your hip isn't hurting quite so much?'

He nodded, and put down a pencil and chose a different colour. Jade looked at the picture he was colouring in.

'Aren't you clever? You've made a beautiful picture. I like the castle and the grass and trees all around.'

'And the birds in the sky,' he pointed out.

'Oh, yes, we mustn't forget the birds, and that wonderful yellow sun. It's lovely colouring.' She looked at the teddy bear, tucked in beside him in the bed. 'And how's Toby doing?'

He put down his pencil and pulled the teddy bear from beneath the covers. He held him up in front of him with both hands, examining him carefully. 'He still has his banjin on,' he said, pointing to the white bandage on the bear's leg. 'It can't come off, 'cos his leg's still poorly. His leg won't go up like mine, so he has to keep it straight.'

'Yes, I see that—but I think he'll be all right as long as he rests next to you.'

He nodded and gave the bear a hug. 'He likes being with me. When Mummy gets back with her coffee, I'm going to give him some of my drink.'

'I'm sure he'll love that.' Jade smiled and after a minute or two she left him to get on with his colouring. She'd examine him again when his leg was out of traction in an hour or so but, from what she could see at the moment, he was doing fine. Inside, a little flicker of happiness sparked into flame. It was good to know that some things were going her way.

She went in search of Ben. He would be tending to the eight-year-old girl who had been admitted a few days ago, and apart from wanting to be with Ben once more she was keen to know how the young girl was getting on.

He gave her a brief smile as she approached the bed-side.

'Hi, there.' She returned the smile and gave Mandy, the nurse who was assisting him, a friendly nod. 'How's she doing?' The child's eyes were closed. She was listless and pale, worn out from all the stomach cramps, vomiting and diarrhoea that had racked her body over the last few days.

He frowned. 'She's very poorly,' he said, keeping his voice low so that the child would not hear. 'The bacteria lodged in her digestive system and formed toxins that are destroying her red blood cells. Now her kidneys are failing.' He had set up a saline drip some time ago to help maintain the child's normal salt and water levels, and now he was taking her blood pressure.

'I'm going to prescribe an antihypertensive medication,' he told Mandy a moment later. 'And I think we're going to have to consider blood transfusions—packed red blood cells and platelets.' He turned to Jade. 'I'll have to check with the consultant, of course, but that would seem to be the best course of action to correct the anaemia. He might want to consider plasma exchange, to filter out the antibodies that are part of the problem.' He glanced at the sleeping girl, his expression serious. 'This has all come on so suddenly.'

Jade nodded. She could see why he was worried. The child's heart rate was very fast, and her breathing was laboured, both signs of severe anaemia.

'Is there anything I can do?'

'You could talk to the parents, if you like. I've already explained the situation to them, but it never hurts to give extra support.' He checked the monitors and Jade noticed that the girl's blood-oxygen level was very low. 'The plasma exchange usually works well, but it takes quite a while. I've a feeling the renal consultant will want her to have dialysis to clean out the toxins—

that will probably be best done at a specialist hospital in Liverpool, near to where she lives.' He winced. 'Apparently the family were enjoying a week in London when this happened.'

'It's so sad.'

'Yes, it is.'

Jade glanced through the child's file, and then went to find the parents, as he'd suggested, to see if she could answer any questions they might have.

It was only later, when things were relatively quiet and it was about time for an afternoon break, that she decided it might be the right moment to seek Ben out and give him the cake she'd made for him.

She hurried to fetch the cake tin from her locker, and then went in search of him, checking each of the paediatric bays in turn, but he was nowhere to be found.

'Are you looking for someone?' Greg asked, looking up from the desk where he was signing lab test forms.

'Yes. I'm trying to find Ben. I have to give him something.'

He glanced at the cake tin. 'The something that's in that tin?'

She nodded. 'It's just a thank you because he helped me out the other day.'

'Oh, I see.' He smiled. 'I think you'll find him in the office. He had to phone the lab to check on some results, and then he was going to write up some notes.'

'Great, thanks for that, Greg.'

She headed for the office. The door was ajar, and she stepped into the room, ready to greet Ben with a smile. Only he wasn't alone in there, she discovered. He was talking to Mandy in a voice that was soft and barely audible, and he had his arms around her. Mandy was looking up at him, but Jade couldn't see her expression. She only knew that Ben looked earnest.

Jade began to back out of the room. Her head was reeling from the shock, and she felt as though somebody had punched her hard in the chest. She was desperately unhappy. Her bubble of joy had burst in an instant. What was he doing with his arms around Mandy?

'Jade—did you want something?' Ben looked up, stepping back from the nurse, as if all was perfectly normal. 'What is it?'

Jade shook her head and put her hand up as if to say it was nothing. She couldn't speak right then, for the life of her, she couldn't find the words, and pride insisted that he shouldn't know she was upset. Instead, she hurried away, her eyes blinded with the sheen of tears. She felt stupid. How could she have let herself be duped in such a way? All of his words, his kisses were meaningless.

The phone in the office rang, and she guessed he had stopped to answer it, because he didn't come after her. It was just as well, because she had nothing to say to him. It took all she had for her to keep going, to do her job and check on her patients. She was glad when the end of her shift finally came and she could escape.

Arriving back at the house, she realised that her ordeal wasn't over. She would still have to face him when they all sat down together for the evening meal. How was she going to cope with that?

Maybe she would just act as though nothing had

happened. She left the cake tin on the worktop in the kitchen and went up to her room.

When she went downstairs an hour or so later, Lucy was serving dinner. 'So how did you enjoy your cake?' she was asking Ben.

'Cake?' he echoed.

'The one that Jade made for you.' She looked at him in surprise. 'You can't have forgotten? It was only this afternoon that she gave it to you.'

Ben shook his head. 'I'm sorry—I don't know what you're talking about. There was no cake.'

Lucy frowned and glanced at the cake tin on the worktop at the side of the room. Placing the last of the hot vegetable dishes on the table, she went over to the tin and opened it up. 'That's strange. I know she took it with her.' She brought the cake over to the table. 'She made it especially for you, as a thank-you for helping her out the other day.'

By that time Jade had come fully into the room, and Ben turned to look at her. 'You made this for me? It's wonderful…and such a great gesture. Thank you for that, Jade.' He stared at the luscious cake, smiling, and then said, 'Was that why you came to the office? I couldn't understand why you just went away.'

'It wasn't important, and I could see that you were busy.' She sat down at the table, and started to help herself to cottage pie and fresh vegetables, purely as a way to keep busy. Lucy was a good cook, but today she was far too emotional to appreciate the food.

Throughout the meal, Ben was trying to chat with her, but she kept her answers short and noncommittal.

She couldn't talk to him. If she did, if she told him what she was thinking, she risked breaking down in front of everyone, and that would never do, and, anyway, what was the point? What could he say to take away the fact that he'd had his arms around Mandy? His behaviour had turned out to be the same as that of her father and Ewan. Why would he do that to her? Maybe he'd been worried about her getting back together with Ewan, but that was no excuse, was it?

If he could ignore what had happened, then she would do her best to do the same—at least while they were together. She finished her meal and then excused herself from the table and went to get ready for her stint at the café bar.

These last few days she'd lost her way. She'd finally realised how much she cared for him but now she had to put all that behind her. It was over, and it was for the best that they didn't have much to do with one another outside work after all. She told herself these things but her heart wasn't listening. She felt dizzy and sick.

She didn't see him again until the morning. She came out of her bedroom and he stopped her in the passage-way.

'I have to go away for a few days,' he told her. 'The little girl with kidney failure, Maisie—we're taking her to Liverpool by ambulance, Mandy and me, that is. She'll be put on dialysis over there. And after that I'll be staying in Hampshire for the weekend, meeting up with some friends back there. I'll be coming back to London on the afternoon train on Sunday.'

In spite of her decision to avoid him as much as pos-

sible, her stomach lurched at the news that he was going
away. 'I hope Maisie will be all right,' she managed.
'It's really sad to see the little girl looking so ill.'

'Yes, it is. But that's not it—I wanted to talk to you
before I go.' He looked at her intently. 'I know something's wrong, and I don't want to go away without sorting things out between us.'

'There's nothing to sort out.'

He frowned. 'Jade, I know that's not true—I've obviously done something to upset you, and all I can think
is that it started when you came into the office yesterday afternoon. You were okay up until then. All I remember is that I was talking to Mandy at the time.'

She said drily, 'You had your arms around her, as I
recall.'

He looked at her searchingly. 'That's the problem,
isn't it?' He waited a moment, but when she didn't answer, he said, 'It didn't mean anything. I want you to
know that. It wasn't what you think.'

She gave a light shrug. 'You're a free agent,' she
murmured, pretending indifference. 'You can do as you
please.'

'No.' He shook his head. 'You don't understand, Jade.
I mean what I say. It was nothing. I was comforting her,
that's all.'

'Forget it, Ben.' She pulled a face. 'That's the kind
of thing my brothers say, Ross and James, whenever
they're caught out. Believe me, I've heard it all, things
like it was nothing...I didn't know she was coming
over...we met by accident...and so on...and so on.'

'Your brothers are very young. Especially Ross. He's

not likely to settle down any time soon, but I expect your brother James will lose interest in playing the field sooner or later. What you need to remember is that I'm not like your brothers, Jade, and I'm definitely not anything like your father. You just have to trust me.'

'Do I? My father was always telling my mother she was imagining things when she tackled him about his away days. For myself, I've always thought that actions speak louder than words.' She'd seen him with her own eyes. Who did he think he was kidding? Was she going to trust what he said and then be made to look a fool, just as she had when Ewan had 'comforted' Melanie?

He reached for her, his hands lightly clasping her upper arms. 'I don't know why you refuse to believe me. Is this to do with Ewan? You're going to see him this weekend, aren't you? Is that why you're backing away from me...because you're having second thoughts? All this other stuff about Mandy is just an excuse, isn't it?'

'You can think what you like,' she said. 'Perhaps you're the one who's making excuses.'

He frowned, giving an exasperated sigh. 'Look, I have to go, but I want you to understand that I care about you, very much, and I don't want you to be hurt or upset. I wouldn't hurt you for the world. You have to know that.'

Stubbornly, she didn't answer him, and he said in frustration, 'I'll call you.' He checked his watch. 'I have to go, or I'll be late.'

She watched him go, and all she could think was that he was going to be with Mandy. She felt as though her heart was breaking.

At work that day, she discovered that she was to spend her time in the neonatal unit, and she put all her efforts into caring for the newborn baby assigned to her. At the very least, keeping busy helped to push a good many of the unhappy thoughts from her mind. The baby was a tiny little thing, a low birth weight, and she was struggling to breathe because her lungs were filled with fluid.

'Before birth babies' lungs are full of fluid,' the professor explained. 'They don't need to breathe through their lungs at that time, because they receive all the oxygen they need from the placentas. As the birth date comes near, though, hormonal changes mean that the lungs start to clear. Then when the baby is born, her first few breaths will usually finish the job. The fluid is absorbed into the bloodstream or the lymphatic system.'

'But not in this case.'

'That's right. The fluid is clearing too slowly, and so she's breathless and her lungs are having to work much harder to get oxygen.' He pointed out the areas of fluid on the chest X-ray. 'So what we have to do is supply oxygen through a face mask or a plastic oxygen hood over the cot while her lungs gradually clear.'

'What about nutrition? She's breathing so fast, it doesn't look as though she'll be able to feed properly,' Jade pointed out.

'Correct.' The professor beamed. 'So that's where you come in, my dear. You can set up the intravenous line and start giving her fluids to hydrate her and stop her blood sugar from dropping too low.'

Jade swallowed, her mouth suddenly dry. All these techniques were ones she needed to know about for when she was sent out into the world as a junior doctor. Any chance she had to do these procedures was good practice...but this baby was so tiny. Her mind balked at the task ahead, until she told herself that without it, the infant would surely die.

'Are you okay with that?' The professor was looking at her.

'Yes, of course. I'll get started on it right away.'

Some twenty minutes later, it was all finished. The infant was being fed through a tube into a vein, and right now she was nestled cosily in Jade's arm, while with her free hand Jade wafted oxygen into her nostrils through a face-mask.

In a little while the baby would go back into her oxygen tent, but for now, while the infant's mother went to get some lunch, Jade was making the most of the chance to cuddle her. 'You're a little angel,' she murmured softly. 'You hardly made a sound when I set up the drip, and the professor was so pleased. I think I want a baby just like you one day.'

As she sat there, cradling the child, her thoughts meandered to Ben. Where was he? What was he doing?

She had begun to realise just how much she missed him. She felt empty inside, and she didn't know what to do with herself. All day she had waited for his call, but it hadn't come, and her spirits sank even lower.

Had all his fine talk of caring for her been made up of so much hot air? She couldn't rid herself of these feelings of worthlessness and dejection. When her father had left, it had been as though she'd been abandoned, and now she was experiencing those feelings all over again. It was all her own fault for letting herself get close to Ben, wasn't it? She should never have let her guard down because now she was definitely paying the price.

On Saturday she went to meet Ewan, as they'd arranged. She was apprehensive, worried about the outcome of the meeting, but instinct told her it had to be done if she was to ever be able to get on with her life, and so she steeled herself to go through with it.

He was sitting in a discreet corner of the coffee shop, almost hidden by a bamboo screen, but he stood up as she approached his table, and greeted her with a smile.

'Jade, it's good to see you.' He sounded relieved, and she apologised for being a few minutes late.

'I had a last-minute phone call from my mother, which made it a bit of a rush for me to get here.' She'd had butterflies in her stomach all morning, but strangely, almost as soon she saw him, they disappeared.

'That's all right. I was worried in case you found a reason not to turn up here.'

She didn't like to admit that it had crossed her mind. 'I was curious,' she said. 'You've been away for so long, and I was a bit surprised when you said you wanted to see me.' The waitress came to the table and she ordered a coffee. Ewan was nursing a cup already and declined anything else.

'I've never stopped thinking about you,' he said when the waitress had gone. 'We meant a lot to each other, you and I…but I didn't realise that I would miss you so much when I went away. I tried to bury myself in work out in Argentina, but it didn't help.'

She frowned. 'But Melanie was out there with you. Didn't she help to take your mind off things?'

She studied him briefly. His hair was streaked with gold from the Argentinean sun and there were one or two crease lines around his eyes that had not been there before, but otherwise he had not changed.

'Things didn't work out between us,' he said. 'It didn't take me long to realise that you were the only woman for me. I was wrong to leave you. It was a mistake. We were always right for one another, but I was too taken up with my career to see it.'

'I'm not so sure about that.' The waitress brought the coffee she had ordered, and Jade added a spoonful of sugar and lightly stirred the froth. 'Did Melanie come back with you to England?'

He pulled in a sharp breath, as though she had caught him unawares. Then he shook his head. 'She decided to stay on for a few more months. I think she's fallen for one of the doctors out there.'

It was strange, talking to Ewan after all this time. She'd wondered if she might feel something for him once she saw him again, but she was strangely empty inside. They talked for around an hour, and her feelings didn't change. It was very odd.

She'd felt so much for this man, and now she wondered what she had ever seen in him. She took his story about always thinking of her and realising he had made a mistake with a large pinch of salt. Things had gone wrong with Melanie, she guessed, and that was what had spurred him on to get in touch with her again.

They talked about his work in South America and his new job at a hospital on the other side of the city. He was going to be busy, and he had his life mapped out for him—all except for a girlfriend to keep him company.

'I must go,' she said, some time later. 'It's been good to see you again, Ewan. I hope things work out for you now that you're back in London.'

'Is there a chance that you and I could get back to-gether?' he asked, as they walked out onto the street, but she shook her head.

'I'm sorry, but it's over. It was over a long time ago.'

He frowned, then reached forward and kissed her. 'I'm sorry, too,' he said.

They parted company, and she made her way to the café bar where she was due to start her shift. How could it have taken her this long to see how shallow he was? Ewan was a charmer, and when she'd first met him she'd fallen for him, big time. But she had been younger then and ready to be charmed.

As she'd told him, that was over now. The magic had disappeared.

It was late when she arrived home from the café bar, and she was more than ready for bed, but somehow sleep wouldn't come.

Ben had still not phoned, and she wanted desperately to talk to him. Only now did it occur to her that she'd been wrong to send him on his way without giving him a proper chance to explain his actions.

Over the years trust had been a difficult thing for her, but somehow or other she had to learn how to handle it or she would never be able to move on.

CHAPTER NINE

'WHAT'S wrong, Jade? You're like a cat on hot bricks today,' Matt observed, looking up from his laptop as Jade paced the living room the next day. 'You haven't stayed still for a second since you came back from the café bar. Haven't you heard anything from Ben yet?'

Jade frowned. Was it so obvious that she and Ben had something going between them? Make that definitely past tense…had *had* something going. That was the trouble with living in such close quarters with other people…she got on really well with Matt and Lucy, but it was hard to have any kind of private life.

'I'm just fed up with studying,' she said. 'I've been trying to get my head around neonatal infections for the last hour or so, but my brain keeps telling me to give it a rest.'

'Hmm. So he hasn't phoned you, then?'

Her shoulders slumped. Obviously, her attempt at trying to deflect him hadn't worked. Matt wasn't going to be easily fobbed off. She sighed. 'No, he hasn't. He said he would, but there's been nothing from him all weekend. Not that it matters. I expect he's been having

a good time at home with his family and friends and
didn't even think about it.'

She went over to the window and looked out, star-
ing at the small, lawned garden. The azaleas were still
in full bloom, but the tulips had died down and looked
raggedy and forlorn—a bit like the way she felt inside.
She moved restlessly. She was angry, frustrated, sad
and disappointed, all at the same time.

'Seems odd, that. Usually, if he says he's going to do
something, he does it.' Matt closed the lid of his laptop.
'I know what you mean about studying. I've been trying to read up on new trauma techniques, but there's
something disheartening about working on a Sunday.
It feels like it should be a day of rest.'

'Too right.'

'I think I might go and practise a few chords on my
guitar.' He looked at Lucy as he said it, a faint smile
lurking around his mouth.

Lucy was working at a table on the other side of the
room, but now she stopped what she was doing in order
to glower at him. 'I know what you're doing,' she said.
'You're trying to bait me, but I'm not rising to it. Do
your worst—I don't care, I've bought ear plugs.' Then,
ignoring him and looking at Jade, she said, 'What train
did Ben say he would be on?'

'I'm not sure.' Jade shrugged. 'He said he should be
home in time for the evening meal.' She gave a wry
smile. 'According to the rota, it's his turn to cook.'

Lucy frowned. 'Well, it doesn't look as though he's
going to be able to do that. It's getting on for six o'clock
already.'

'Looks like we'll have to order a Chinese takeaway,' Matt said. He grinned and did a high five with Jade. 'My favourite.'

'Mine, too.' She chuckled. 'Don't you just love it when we can't be bothered to cook?'

An hour or so later, after they'd stuffed themselves full of Chinese noodles, bean sprouts and a delicious combination of Chinese vegetables and sweet and sour chicken, there was still no sign of Ben.

She cleared the table, determined to keep busy. She wasn't going to think about it any more. It was exhausting.

Then the house phone rang and her heart gave a funny little leap inside her chest. Could it be Ben, trying to get in touch? She hurried to answer it, but her spirits drooped when she realised it wasn't him.

She cheered up a little, though, when her brother James started to speak.

'Hi, Jade. I wondered…if you're not doing anything this evening, would you like to come along to a pop concert? I managed to get hold of a couple of free tickets. I know it's short notice, but I thought it would be good for us to meet up again—I haven't seen you since last time we were together back home, and that must have been several weeks ago.'

'I'd love it,' she said. 'It's so good to hear from you. It's just what I need to perk me up. Actually, I've not been to a concert for ages and it'll be great to see you again.'

A few minutes later she hurried upstairs to get ready. It would be just the thing to get her out of the house and help her to shake off this strange mood that had fallen on her. She changed into fresh jeans and a slinky top, and added heels and a light touch of make-up and she was ready. Her hair was soft and silky, falling loosely about her shoulders.

'Wow, look at you, all dolled up,' Matt said, giving a low whistle. 'Where are you off to?'

'To a concert with a gorgeous young man,' she said with a smile. It was a great morale boost to know that he thought she looked good. 'He's a real catch, and he thinks the world of me—and he has two tickets for that boy band, the ones who were on TV last week. Who says I don't know how to party?'

Matt laughed, but as Jade turned around she caught sight of Ben, standing in the doorway. She stared at him, open-mouthed for a second or two, the breath catching in her lungs. Of the two of them, though, he was by far the worse off—he looked stunned, as though he'd been hit about the head with something.

What must he have thought of her remarks? She made a desperate effort to pull herself together. 'Hi, Ben,' she said. 'We were expecting you home much earlier than this. I'm really sorry, I can't stop and talk, but I have to go and meet my brother and I'm running a bit late.' She hesitated, realising that it must have sounded as though she was babbling. 'I hope everything went well with the little girl you were taking to hospital, and that you had a good weekend.' She gave him a questioning look, and he nodded.

'Good. I'm glad.' Then she pulled in a deep breath and added, 'I must go. Sorry. Perhaps we can talk later?'

She hurried away, and only when she was clear of the house did she stop to drag a deep breath of air into her lungs.

It was all bravado, her attempt to be natural with him. It grieved her to leave when there were so many questions flying around inside her head. She wanted to be with him, to have him tell her everything was okay, and soothe away all her troubles, but of course it wasn't okay. Her pride was wounded, and hadn't he shown that she couldn't rely on him, no matter what he'd said? Not even a phone call.

She met up with James at the front of the venue, where you could see bronze plaques imprinted with the names and handprints of famous people who had performed there over the years. They hugged one another and walked by the fountains, lit up with multicoloured lights that were reflected on the wall of the building.

James bought popcorn for later on, while Jade bought ice-lollies with ice cream in the middle, and it was like being a child again.

'What brought this on?' she asked, glancing at him. He was tall and lithe, with knock-'em-dead good looks, black hair and clear grey eyes. 'The night out, I mean? Is everything all right with you?'

He nodded, and bit into his lolly. 'I've just finished working on a big advertising project,' he said, 'and I wanted to take some time out.'

'I'm glad you thought of me when you got the tickets,' she said cautiously, 'but knowing you, I'd have expected you to have a girl in tow, and that she'd be the one using the ticket. Don't tell me things have gone wrong in that department?'

He smiled. 'No, everything's fine. Really, I mean it. I've met someone who I think might turn out to be special…we get on really well. But there are times when family comes first, when only my little sister will do.'

'Well, I really appreciate that,' she said. Behind the show of optimism, though, she thought she detected a wistful glimmer in his eyes. 'So, what's happened?' she prodded. 'Tell me all about it.'

He screwed up his face. 'I met up with Dad a couple of weeks ago. I can't put my finger on it, but something's been bothering me ever since.'

Jade let out a slow breath. 'Me, too. I went for coffee with him.'

He looked at her searchingly. 'Do you feel it—this kind of emptiness inside? I can't explain it, but it's been eating me up.'

She nodded. 'I know exactly what you mean. I feel the same way. I have done for a long time.'

He looked relieved. 'I can't get my head around the way things are with him. It's as though he thoroughly screwed us up. Even now, all those years since he left, I'm full of resentment.' He shook his head. 'I don't understand it. You'd think I'd never give him a passing thought, wouldn't you?'

She thought about it, and after a while she said, 'The thing is, he was a strong character back then and for, all his mistakes, he was loving and generous with his time—while he was with us. Perhaps that was why it came as such a shock when he went away.' She sighed.

'I've been going over and over it in my mind just lately. There was something about him last time we spoke, though. He seemed different somehow, more regretful. I almost felt sorry for him.'

Since Ewan had come back, she'd been trying to work out why she had such a lack of faith in the men in her life. Was she right to mistrust Ben because both her father and Ewan had let her down? Up to now James had always played the field, too, so maybe that was another element that added to her view of men.

'Yes, I noticed that. Perhaps that's why we're both raking over old coals. He's stirred something up in us, and all the old vulnerabilities have come back.'

She nodded. 'It's hard to shake them off.'

'What do you think is happening with him? Something must have caused him to change.'

She thought for a while before she answered him. 'I had the impression that he's sorry that he missed a good part of our childhood years. Now that he's older, he's mellowed a bit and he's thinking more about what really matters in life...especially family. After all, he doesn't have any other children. And maybe he's in a more settled relationship now and he's thinking about all the things that went wrong when he was with Mum. Perhaps he thinks he could have done things differently.' Hadn't Ewan reacted in the same way?

'Yes, now I come to think of it, that makes sense to me. I'm pretty sure that's what his problem is.' He glanced at her. 'Do you think we should make an effort to see him a bit more often?'

'That would be a good idea.'

They walked inside the building to the seating area, where people were getting ready for the warm-up group. 'I sometimes worry that I might have inherited his faults,' James confided. 'Genetics, you know.'

She looked at him, her eyes filled with sympathy. 'That's a heavy burden to carry around, but I don't think you should let it hold you back. Think of the good things that are going on in your life. Didn't you say you had met someone special?'

She studied him. 'I don't think you're anything like him, James…not when I think back to how you are with people. Yes, you've been out with lots of girls, but I don't believe you ever really hurt anyone, did you?'

'Not intentionally. I was just enjoying life, and the girls were sweet, but sometimes I think they expected too much from me. They wanted something I wasn't prepared to give.'

'Like love, you mean?' She smiled. 'Perhaps all your wild days were just a build-up to finding the real thing. You're the only one in charge of your destiny. You can keep it special—you can make up your mind that you're not going to waste your chances in life, that you're not going to be like him.'

He laid an arm around her shoulders. 'I knew I could rely on you to make me see the light. I'll have to introduce you to Amy some time soon. You'll like her. She's quiet and funny and she keeps my feet on the ground.'

He grinned, his tone light, as though he had cast off a great weight. 'So how's it going at the hospital? Are you managing to keep all those little kiddies in good shape?'

After that, the evening was a great success. The band was lively and Jade's ears were still ringing with the sound of their music, her eyes dazzled by the laser lights and special effects, when she arrived back at the house in the early hours of the morning. She went up to her room as quietly as she could, and fell into a deep sleep soon after.

'Still suffering the after-effects of last night?' Ben asked, when she met up with him in the neonatal unit next morning. He'd left the house way before she'd been up and about. Now he was reading through the notes on a baby that had just been admitted into isolation.

'Does it show?' She blinked. She hoped it didn't, but the truth was she'd had to drag herself out of bed at what had seemed like an unearthly hour that morning in order to get to work on time, and even a quick shower hadn't been enough to blow away the cobwebs.

'It's just that you look very pale. Did you have a good time?'

'Yes, it was great. I don't get to see my brother all that often, so I didn't want to miss out on the chance.' She shrugged. 'I expect I'll be fine after the coffee break.' She sent him a thoughtful glance, and then decided to say what was on her mind. 'Anyway, let's not go into what I've been up to—what happened to you over the weekend? Didn't you say you were going to call me? And how come you were so late getting back? What happened? Did something more interesting come up?'

'I did call you.' His grey-blue eyes watched her steadily. 'Two or three times, in fact, but for some reason my calls weren't getting through. Have you checked your phone lately? Maybe something happened when it was lying on the grass overnight.'

She sucked in her breath. 'I thought you'd forgotten all about me.' She quickly checked her phone. 'Funny, that—I've noticed some odd things happening with it lately. And I thought it was strange that I haven't been getting any calls. I've been banging it every now and again when the screen blanks off, and that seemed to do the trick.'

She bit her lip. In her mind she'd been accusing him of abandoning her, and all the time he'd been perfectly innocent. She looked at him, wide eyed. 'Maybe the battery's not making a good connection.'

'Maybe.' His brows drew together. 'Why would I forget all about you? I told you how much I care about you. Did you think I was making it up?'

'I—it crossed my mind.' She faltered, wrongfooted, but then a thought occurred to her and her chin went up in a direct challenge. 'Anyway, you could have used the landline.'

'And have Matt and Lucy listen in?' His tone was scornful. 'I don't think so.'

In spite of herself, she laughed. 'There is that, I suppose.' She was quiet for a moment or two. 'I was imagining all sorts of things—and then when you didn't come home at the time you said you would, I didn't know what to think.'

He frowned. 'There was a problem on the train line. Something was blocking the track, debris of some sort, and the driver had to slam on the brakes. We were stuck on the line for a couple of hours.'

She gasped. 'Oh, no…were you hurt? Oh…and all the time I was thinking…' She reached out to him, laying her hand on his arm, wanting to hold him and make sure that he was all right.

'I'm fine. A bit of a headache left over from the whiplash effect, but other than that I'm okay.'

She wanted to lay her hand on his brow and soothe his pain. It was frustrating to know that they were at work and there were people about who might come along at any minute and disturb them.

'And the other passengers, how were they—you mentioned whiplash, so it must have been quite bad?'

He laid down the notes he'd been studying and picked up a batch of lab-test results. 'People were thrown about a bit, and there were some minor injuries. I did what I could. I helped out with some of the passengers who had sprained their wrists and so on, holding onto rails to keep themselves from falling. We found some first-aid boxes in the carriages.'

She shook her head. 'I can't believe you were going through all that, and I knew nothing about it. I'm so sorry. I'm sorry for what you went through, and for doubting you.'

He gave her an assessing glance. 'You know, Jade, your problem is you don't have any faith in people. You have to learn to trust me.' A muscle flicked in his jaw. 'You have to see me for who I am, not who you think I am.'

He seemed to be annoyed with her, and Jade couldn't

really blame him for that. All her life she'd been in the shadow of her father and his actions, and it had co-loured everything. Could she learn to trust? She'd seen her mother suffer badly and she was so afraid of being hurt.

'Anyway, let's go and see to this baby in the isolation ward,' he said, becoming brisk and efficient. 'She's ten days old, and her mother went down with chickenpox four days before the baby was delivered.'

Jade winced. 'That's bad, isn't it? The timing's all wrong, the worst.'

'Yes, it is. It means the baby got the virus while still in the womb, but she was born before she could receive any antibodies from the mother. That makes for a really bad outcome, unless we can get things under control.'

They went over to the ward, and Jade spoke to the baby's mother while Ben examined the infant.

'Is my baby going to be all right?' The mother was young, nineteen years old, and desperately protective of her child. She was ill herself, suffering badly with the illness which, when contracted by a small child, would follow a mild course, but was much more severe in an adult.

Jade wanted to reassure the woman but she knew that in cases such as these, the outcome wasn't always good. There could be complications, and in such a young child they could be fatal.

'We're doing everything we can to take care of her,' she said in a soothing voice. 'The problem we have is the risk of complications such as pneumonia. In such a small baby that can be very serious, so we have to take every step we can to keep ahead of the disease.'

She spoke to the mother for a little longer, but although she tried to keep a positive attitude, Jade knew that Ben was very concerned for this tiny child.

'Her temperature's unstable,' he said quietly when she went over to him by the baby's cot. The infant was inside an oxygen tent because her blood-oxygen level was low and getting lower. 'It's not looking good,' he went on. 'Her lungs are filling up, her airways are compromised, and she's beginning to look very ill. I'm worried that there may be some secondary infection.'

'So you'll take blood samples?'

'Yes, I've already done it, along with mucus and sputum samples. I've asked the lab to deal with them urgently. Up to now there's been no point in giving her antibiotics. They simply won't work if it's a viral infection.'

It was upsetting. The infant was fretful, her cry thin and thready, and she was such a frail little thing it was hard to see how she could fight this. Her breathing was rapid, and that was not a good sign. She was wheezing and coughing, all signs adding up to the worst diagnosis.

'You're treating her with acyclovir?' Jade asked.

'That's right.' He nodded. 'It won't cure the virus, but it should stop it in its tracks. But from the looks of things, her lungs are already affected, and that means we have a problem on our hands. We'll suction her mouth and nose to clear the thick secretions and try to make her more comfortable, and we'll give her medicine to bring down her temperature. I'll ask Alice, the nurse, to go on treating the rash with medication to ease the itching.' He pulled a face. 'In the meantime, all we can do is see that she gets plenty of fluids and wait for the results of the tests.'

He wrote up the instructions for the nurse, and then went to speak to the baby's mother. Jade excused herself and went to check up on the other patients assigned to her, both in Neonatal and Paediatrics. The baby was the difficult part of her job, the side of it where the outcome could go either way, and it grieved her that bad news might be something she had to learn to accept.

One good aspect of the work was that patients like four-year-old Tim often made a quick and complete recovery. Tim wasn't quite at that stage yet, but when she went to see him, his hip pain had almost gone.

'I don't want my leg up in that lift thingy, any more,' he told her. 'It's all right now. I don't need it to be up.'

'I'm really glad to hear that, Tim,' she said with a smile. 'It's good to know that you're feeling better.'

'I am.' He nodded. Then, with a hopeful expression, he asked, 'Can I get up and play with the toys over there in the corner?'

Jade gave it some thought. It was best for him to stay off the leg for a while longer, to give it the best chance of healing completely, but once a child started to get restless, it was difficult to keep him bed-bound.

'You know, Tim, I think it would be better for you to keep off that leg for just a little while longer—but I can bring some of the toys over to you, if you like. And maybe later today Mandy will help you over there so that you can play for a little while. We'll do it just a little bit at a time, if that's all right with you?'

'Okay.' He pointed to the small plastic building bricks. 'I want to play with those. Can I?'

'Yes, I'll get them for you. I'll pull the bedside table over to you so that you can use it.' Her mouth curved. 'And I'll pop back later to see how you're getting on with them.'

She left him after a few minutes, and went over to the office to write up her notes. The morning had gone quickly and it was already getting on for lunchtime. After a while, Ben came to join her in the office, half sitting on the table and reaching for the phone.

'I'm going to phone the Liverpool hospital to find out how Maisie is doing,' he said. 'It's been a few days now since she went on dialysis, so I'm hoping she's on the mend.'

Jade watched him. It was one of the wonderful things about him, the way he thought about the children in his care. He didn't just treat them, he followed up, wanting to make sure that they were all right, even when they were no longer his responsibility.

He put his hand over the mouthpiece a moment later, and told her, 'She's doing okay.' He went back to his conversation with the nurse at the other end of the line. 'Thanks for that,' he said. 'You've been really helpful.'

He replaced the receiver and then looked at Jade. 'She'll be on dialysis for another week at least, but they're hopeful that she's reached a turning point. All the signs are that she's getting over the infection.'

'That's brilliant news. I know how worried you were about her.'

'I was.' He stood up. 'Have you finished for the morning? Shall we go and get some lunch? We could walk to the park by Tower Bridge and watch the boats go by. It's only a few minutes away.'

'That sounds good.'

They bought salad and bread rolls from the cafeteria, along with fruit buns and polystyrene cups of coffee, and then they strolled out into the afternoon sunshine. The park was alongside the river, and as they approached this oasis of green, the lopsided glass dome of City Hall rose up in front of them. Nearby was Tower Bridge, magnificent against the skyline.

They chose a spot in the park where they could sit on the grass and watch the world go by at their leisure.

It felt good to be there with Ben. She didn't know whether she'd ruined everything between them, but he seemed relaxed and he'd wanted to be there with her, and that was enough for the moment.

After they'd eaten, they cleared everything away and deposited the rubbish in a litter-bin nearby. Ben took her hand and they walked by the river for a while, and Jade revelled in that close, warm contact. She loved the feel of the soft breeze on her skin, the smell of the newly mown grass, and the colours all around seemed brighter than ever before. The blossom on the trees was a pure, pristine white, and silver birch trees rose majestically, reaching skywards. It all seemed like heaven to her just then.

'I thought about you all weekend,' he said. They'd

reached the herbaceous gardens, and here the colour was even more vibrant. Perhaps she was seeing things this way because all her senses were heightened now that she was alone with him.

'Did you?' She was quiet, thinking about that. 'I thought about you, but I was anxious because you were with Mandy.'

'Why would that bother you? She was there to take care of the little girl.'

'But I saw you with your arms around her. I know you said it was nothing, but it was to me. I was shocked and hurt.'

'Mandy was upset that day. She was worried about the little girl who'd gone into kidney failure. The child was going downhill all the time, and Mandy had spent so many hours with her. I tried to tell her that her best chance was with dialysis, but nothing was certain, and I suppose the thought that she would be going away and we'd perhaps lose track of her made matters worse. She'll be glad to know that the child is on the mend.'

'Oh, I see.'

'I told you that you need to trust me.'

'Yes, but look at it from my point of view,' Jade murmured. 'How would you feel if the situation was reversed?'

He frowned. 'How do you think I felt when you said you were going to see your ex-boyfriend? I've had to think about that all weekend, wondering whether you were going to take him back.'

She shook her head. 'That's not going to happen. I saw him and I realised that there was never anything there between us. It was never love. I thought it was, but...'

She didn't get to finish the sentence. He stopped in mid-stride and took her into his arms, kissing her fiercely. He didn't seem to care that they were out in the open, in full view of anyone who happened to stroll around the bend in the walkway. And after a moment or two she didn't care much either. All she could think about was that his mouth had claimed hers, and his hands were pressuring her to him as if he couldn't get enough of her.

His breathing was ragged, and she loved that. Her heart swelled with the knowledge that she could do that to him, that he could feel such passion, such desire for her. She wound her hands around the back of his neck, her body moving against him, wanting him, needing him.

'I want you,' he muttered in a roughened voice. 'Only you. You were on my mind the whole time. And then when I came back and you told Matt you were going out with another man, I was insanely jealous.'

'I told you he was my brother,' she said cautiously. 'Didn't you believe me?'

He nodded. 'Yes, but for that instant I felt pure shock and unbelievable hurt.'

She smiled. 'I hate to say it, but at least now you know how it feels when the boot's on the other foot.' She looked up at him, her green eyes sparkling with mischief, and with something else, too. There was love in the way she gazed at him. It came on her suddenly that this was the one man she could spend the rest of her life with—the one man she could love.

He kissed her again, fiercely, possessively, and she was burning, aching with need. She clung to him, ran her arms over his strong, powerful biceps, loving the feel of him. He meant everything to her. This last weekend had shown her just how much she needed him. Her life would be empty without him.

And yet the realisation weighed heavily on her. Even now, that thread of caution held her back. He'd said he needed her and cared for her, but he'd never mentioned the word love. He was red-blooded and fired up, and that was driving him right now, and she was full of joy, but how long would it last? What was it James had said...? 'They wanted more than I could give.'

She wanted much more. Ben had said he missed her, wanted her, but in all this time he had never uttered the precious words she wanted to hear.

She looked into his eyes. Desire burned like flame in those dark depths. Would that be enough to sustain them?

She didn't say anything of what was in her mind. They were both raw, their feelings exposed, vulnerable, and perhaps she would just wait to see what happened.

'I could stay here for evermore,' he murmured, but then he added with a sigh, 'but I think it's time we were heading back towards the hospital.'

She nodded and, hand in hand, they started back along the way they had come.

They each had their own work to tend to at the hospital, but at the end of the afternoon Jade went in search of Ben once more. Her shift had finished, but he was still on duty, and it looked as though he had been going non-stop since they'd come back from lunch.

He was frowning, trying to work out the dosage of medicine for one of the tiny babies in his care. His hair was tousled where he'd been running his hands through it, and she wondered if he was finding things tough. Even so, he looked incredibly sexy. He was flat stomached, dark trousers moulding his strong legs, his shirtsleeves pushed up to reveal those lightly tanned forearms.

'It looks as though things have been pretty hectic for you around here,' she murmured, as soon as he'd finished checking the calculation.

'We've had a few admissions,' he agreed, 'so I've been running between Neonatal and Paediatrics for the last few hours. I've had some seriously sick children on my hands.'

She frowned. 'Where's the senior house officer? And Professor Farnham?'

'The professor's away at a conference, and the registrar's busy on the surgical ward. As for the senior house officer, he went off duty a couple of hours ago, and his replacement has called in sick. The powers that be are trying to bring in a locum, but it's a bit late in the day and they've not been having too much luck up to now.'

'So you've had to handle everything on your own? And they talk about making things easier for junior doctors.' She laid a hand on his shoulder, loving the way the warmth of his body permeated through to her, and she wished she could put her arms around him and hug him. Instead, she said, 'Have you managed to get a break yet? You must have been on the go for hours.'

'Not yet. It's been one thing after another.'

She looked at him, and the mound of paperwork he had to get through. He had to write up case notes, check X-ray films and scans, read reports and lab-test results. And that was without counting the number of checks he had to make on patients. 'I'll be back in a minute,' she said.

By the time she came back, he was bending over a cot, playing with one of the babies, putting his finger out for him to hold and laughing softly when the infant's legs came up to him, trying to reach him with his feet at the same time as his hands.

Jade smiled, watching him. Then he stepped back and removed the stainless-steel tray with the syringe that he must have used to medicate the infant. 'He'll be all right, I think,' he told Jade as he cleared away. 'He's responding pretty well to treatment.'

'That's good.' Her voice was soft as she placed a tray on the table just to one side of the treatment bay. 'I've raided the fridge and brought you some tea and sandwiches,' she said. 'Eat them now, before you do anything else. You need to keep up your energy.'

'Thanks.' He beamed her a smile. 'I don't know how I've managed without you up till now. Since you came along, things have definitely started to look up.'

He stood by the table and bit into a sandwich, savouring it. 'Mmm...that's good.' Then he swallowed the tea thirstily, as though he hadn't had a drink in hours.

When he'd finished, he reached for her and drew her

alongside him. 'I should take you out somewhere special,' he murmured. 'You really enjoyed that concert,
didn't you? Perhaps we should do something tonight
when I'm finished here.'

'Which will be in about an hour, won't it?'

He nodded.

'Hmm.' She studied him thoughtfully. 'Actually, you
look as though a night out is the very last thing you
need. You must have come on duty at an impossible
hour this morning, and there are shadows under your
eyes.'

He gave a wry smile. 'One of the hazards of being a
junior doctor.'

'Tell you what,' she said, coming to a quick decision,
'why don't I cook us a meal tonight? Matt and Lucy will
both be out, so we'll have the house to ourselves. Matt's
doing a gig till the early hours, and Lucy is spending the
night with relatives—her cousin has come to London
for a few days, so they're having a get-together.'

'A night in…just the two of us…that sounds like
something I could really look forward to,' he said, his
gaze moving over her. He brushed her mouth with a
kiss and sent tingling sensations to flow in a tidal wave
through her body. 'Are you sure you don't mind cooking?'

She absorbed the heady thrill of his body next to
hers. 'I don't mind. What would you like…steaks, spa-
ghetti, paella? I know they're all your favourites.'

'Steak sounds good.' His hand rested on her hip,
warming her through and through.

'Then steak it shall be.' She kissed him lightly on

the forehead and reluctantly eased herself away from him. 'I'll go home and get things ready. I'll see you in an hour, then?'

'An hour, yes.'

She was walking on air all the way home, and she still hadn't subsided when she'd finished her preparations and it was time to lay the table. She picked out a white damask tablecloth, and then she buffed up wine glasses until they shone. There was a bottle of red wine on the sideboard. In an afterthought, she borrowed the candelabra from the table in the hallway and set them down in the middle of the table. Soft lights, romantic music and good food...what more could they want?

Everything was ready in the kitchen, waiting for Ben to come home so that she could start the meal. It would be wonderful—their first evening truly alone, just the two of them. She couldn't wait. She'd changed into a pretty cotton top and a skirt that gently flowed around her calves, and her hair was held back with small enamelled clips in a softly feminine style.

Now all she needed was for Ben to arrive. She looked at the clock. He was already an hour late. And there had been no phone call to explain the delay, nothing at all. Even if her phone was playing up, he could use the landline now that he knew Matt and Lucy were out.

But he didn't do that. Two hours after he had promised to be home she was pacing the floor as she had on Sunday. Where was he? Why wasn't he here? She looked at the phone, willing it to ring, but still nothing happened. Not a sound.

Why would he have let her down?

She thought she had finally learned what made him tick, but now she was in that same position all over again, wondering why he hadn't come home. There was that familiar sick feeling starting up in her stomach... the feeling of being unwanted, let down, deserted.

CHAPTER TEN

ANOTHER half-hour went by and still Jade heard nothing from Ben. She frowned. She was sitting at the table, willing the kitchen door to open and for him to walk in, but it didn't happen.

Could he have been in another accident? Surely not? Perhaps he had found something or someone more interesting, and he'd changed his mind about coming back to her? A drink after work, perhaps, with friends, who just happened to cajole him into going along with them to a bar?

No. She stood up, angry with herself for thinking that way. He wouldn't do that to her. There had to be a more reasonable explanation. Once and for all, she had to conquer her fears and believe in him.

She went over to the phone and dialled the hospital's switchboard. Perhaps he was still there.

A few minutes later, after the switchboard operator had confirmed her thoughts, she was on her way to the hospital. She went by bus this time so as to get there sooner, and the minute it dropped her off outside the building, she hurried over to Neonatal.

She found Ben in the isolation room, where the infant

with neonatal varicella, the chickenpox virus, was being treated. The mother wasn't around, and she guessed she must have been taken to X-Ray or some other department for tests.

'Jade, sweetheart, what are you doing here?' Ben looked up from the baby's cot, surprise and pleasure flitting across his face.

'I came to see what had happened to you. You were so late, and you didn't call.'

'I'm sorry. I haven't been able to get away to use the office phone, not even for a minute, and there's sensitive equipment round here so using the mobile wasn't an option. I haven't been able to get hold of anyone to ring for me.'

She nodded. 'I guessed as much.'

He smiled. 'You did? I've been worrying, imagining you were thinking all sorts of things because I'd let you down.'

All the time he was talking, he continued to work with the baby. He was adding medication to the infant's intravenous line—as far as Jade could see, he was giving her antibiotics.

'Not this time,' she said. 'I learned a valuable lesson the other day. I realised that I have to put my trust in you, so I've made up my mind that I'll always give you the benefit of the doubt from now on.' She smiled. 'Woe betide you if you mess me about, though.'

'I won't be doing that.' He didn't smile. He looked at her, his grey-blue eyes sincere, and she was still for a while, absorbing the steady, clear-cut message he was sending her.

Then he straightened and checked the monitors. The readings weren't good…low blood-oxygen, high respiratory rate, rapid heartbeat. This infant was in a bad way.

'You should have stayed at home,' he chided her. 'You work hard enough as it is, and you need to take advantage of any opportunity you get to relax.'

'As if I could do that when you didn't come home.'

He pulled a face. 'I'm sorry about that. Young Becky, here, started having seizures, and I had to act quickly. Her mother begged me to stay and take care of her—for some reason she has a lot of confidence in me—and, anyway, I couldn't pass her over to someone else who would have to come up to speed with the case. To be honest, I wanted to see this one through. She's so tiny, so frail, and I can't lose her. I won't lose her. I'm going to stay until she turns the corner.'

His dedication brought a lump to Jade's throat. She said quietly, 'The tests must have come back—does she have a secondary infection?'

'Unfortunately, yes. The results came in not long after we spoke this morning, so I started her on antibiotics straight away. I'm doing everything I can for her, but her chest is so congested, and I have to keep using suction on her nose and mouth to try to keep her airways clear.' Even as he spoke, he was preparing to use the suction equipment once again. 'There aren't any nurses available to help out—we're short-staffed, and this couldn't have happened at a worse time.'

'Let me do that,' Jade said. 'You look all in. Go and

sit down or, better still, lie down and try and get some rest. I'll watch over her for you.'

He pulled in a deep breath, and she knew he was trying to work out whether he could afford to let go. 'I'll turn her over to you if I think she's taking a turn for the worse,' she promised him.

'Okay. Just for a little while, then.' He glanced once more at the baby, and then went over to the treatment couch and stretched out there. 'I'll just rest for a minute or two.'

He'd decided she could be trusted with the baby that was so precious to him, and the knowledge caused a warm swell of pride to rise up in her. He watched her for a minute or two as she carefully cleared the infant's airways, and after a while his eyes gradually closed. He'd fallen asleep.

Jade loosened Becky's garments and applied a soothing lotion to the rash. 'You're not a happy little soul, are you?' she said softly, when she'd finished. 'How about I pick you up and see if we can clear your chest a bit?'

She lifted the infant up and positioned her carefully so that she lay across her shoulder, and then she turned so that the child's nose and mouth were close to the opening in the oxygen tent. That way she would still be able to breathe in the life-giving oxygen.

Gently, she patted the little girl's back, enjoying the feel of this tiny, soft little bundle draped over her chest. The infant snuffled and coughed and squirmed for a while, but eventually she settled, and Jade realised that she, too, had fallen asleep.

'Well, there we are, both of you slumbering away

like peaceful angels.' She smiled to herself. This was not quite the evening she'd envisaged, but somehow she felt incredibly calm and satisfied.

Ben woke with a small start some time later when a trolley clattered by in the corridor outside. He blinked. 'What did I miss? Is everything all right?' Then, as his brain cleared, he looked at Jade and the baby, an arrested look in his eyes.

'You look so content, the pair of you,' he said in wonder. 'She's well away—and from the looks of things, she's improving a little.' He was checking out the monitors, and it was true. The blood-oxygen levels had risen slightly, and both her breathing and heart rate were a bit lower than before.

'I guess the antibiotics must have started to kick in. How many doses has she had?'

'A couple.' He came over to them and gently stroked the sleeping baby's fine hair. 'The change of position must have done her good as well.'

'And maybe she needed a cuddle.'

'Hmm. She's not the only one.' He gave her a roguish smile. 'I'm really glad you came over here. It's been good having you around.'

She gave him an answering smile, easing her position so that she could sit back a little more comfortably and lightly rub the baby's back. 'Funny, that…I've been thinking the same thing about you.'

The baby coughed and made a soft little burp, then yawned and snuggled into Jade's shoulder once more, and they both laughed. 'Well, now she's a lot more comfortable.'

He watched her as she gently stroked the tiny infant. 'You look very content, doing that. It's not quite what we had in mind for this evening, is it? But I'm glad you're not cross with me for staying on here. I'm glad you understand.'

'I'm sure I'd have done the same thing if the positions had been reversed. Anyway, that's what we came into medicine for, isn't it…to do what we could to save lives?'

'Yes.' He smiled. 'But I was looking forward to spending time with you at the house, just the two of us.'

'Me, too. But maybe we can still do that.' She turned her head a little so that she could see the sleeping baby's face. 'I don't know if it's my imagination, but it seems to me her breathing is a little easier.'

'I think you're right. I've a feeling the panic might be over where she's concerned. Perhaps we got the antibiotics to her just in time…along with all the other treatments we've been giving her, she seems to be responding better than I expected.' He laid the back of his hand lightly against the baby's cheek. 'Perhaps we should pop her back in her cot. I'll page the registrar to come and take over here, and then I can take you home.'

'Okay. Will her mother be coming back soon?'

'I imagine so.' He texted a message to the registrar. 'She had some chest problems, so a nurse took her to get an X-ray. It's nothing serious, but we want to make sure we can nip any infection in the bud as early as possible. She'll be pleased to see that Becky's not fretful any more. It's a sign she's doing better.'

'It must be a worrying time for her.' Jade got to her

feet, and laid the baby carefully in her cot, making sure that she was comfortable and that the oxygen flowed freely around her. 'Sleep tight, little one,' she murmured.

Ben reached for her. 'It feels so good to be with you.' He kissed her tenderly. 'Everything seemed to change for me after you came into my life. I didn't understand what was happening to me, at first, but then I realised I wanted to be with you, more and more. I've never felt like that before, with any woman. I hated the thought that you might be with someone else.'

Her eyes widened. Could he really be saying what she'd longed to hear? But there was no chance to say anything more, to ask all the questions that crowded into her head, because the registrar pushed open the door and Ben gently released her.

'You've been here way too long,' he told Ben. He looked at them oddly, as though he sensed something in the air. 'I'll take over from you now.'

He looked at the baby, and then checked the monitors and glanced through the baby's file. 'And don't worry about this infant, I'll take very special care of her.'

'Good. I've been worried by how ill she was.' Ben frowned. 'I didn't want to leave until I felt sure that it was safe, that she was going to be all right.'

The registrar looked at them both once more, a faint smile touching his mouth. 'I think you'll be all right to get yourselves off home,' he said. 'The baby's responding to the antibiotics and oxygen therapy—she's looking a lot better than she did this morning. I've seen a lot of these cases over the years—once they've passed through that critical stage, they start to improve day by day. She's clearly over the worst, now. Anyway, you've done a great job here and, to be honest, you look as though you need to be somewhere else.'

Ben smiled. 'Maybe you're right. Thanks. We'll be off, then.' He didn't wait any longer but held open the door for Jade, and together they walked out of the hospital.

'Do you want to take the bus and get home quicker, or do you feel like walking for a bit?' he suggested. 'I thought, if you were up for it, maybe we could take the long route home, and walk by the river. I think it might help to clear my head.'

'That sounds like a good idea.'

'Good.' He linked hands with her, her hand lost in his bigger one, and they walked in companionable silence for a while. Darkness had fallen by now, and the sounds of the city were all around them, with people going into the bars or spilling out of the theatre.

Then they came to the river, and stopped in a secluded place to watch the moonlight shimmering on the water. In the distance, tall buildings were silhouetted against the night sky, the city lights blazing, and it felt to Jade as though there was magic in the air.

She said huskily, 'Did you mean what you said back at the hospital? About everything changing for you?'

'I did.' He was silent for a second or two, thinking, and then he said softly, 'It feels right, somehow, seeing you every day, being in the same house, sitting down to an evening meal together. And then at work my whole world seems brighter whenever you're close by.'

'I felt the same way,' she confessed. 'I wasn't sure how it would be when you first moved in. I really liked you, but I was afraid of getting too close. And then, when I got to know you better, I couldn't help myself, even against my better judgement I wanted to be with you more and more. I hated it when you went away.'

'Did you?' His eyes widened. 'That's good to know.' He smiled. 'More than good. I know it's been a huge stumbling block for you, letting yourself get involved with me. You've always put up barriers.' He put an arm around her shoulders.

'Yes.' She knew she needed to explain. She felt guilty, because he'd always been considerate and under-standing, and perhaps he hadn't deserved to be treated as though he was devil-may-care and irresponsible. 'I've always been so afraid of getting involved, I thought I was bound to be hurt, but you were right the other day when you said I should see you for who you are, and not who I think you are. I've realised that you're noth-ing like Ewan or my father.'

'Your father's way of going on clouded everything, didn't it?'

'Yes, it did, and it made what happened with Ewan seem far worse. But I think my father has mellowed. He seems to have had a change of heart, and I think he's beginning to realise that he let go of something precious. I didn't get it at first, but then I talked things over with my brother, and I knew that seeing my father again had given me hope.'

He drew in a deep breath. 'Does that mean you're willing to give us a chance? Now you've seen how

things really are, perhaps we can make a go of it...
perhaps you'll have faith in me and believe me when I
tell you that you matter to me more than anyone.' She
nodded, and he gave a sigh of relief. 'All I know is I've
never felt this way before.' He bent his head to kiss her
gently. 'I love you, Jade. I love everything about you,
the way you care about people, how you spend time
with the babies and children and try to make them feel
good.'

He smiled. 'I love the way you manage to stay calm
and unfazed by most things. And you have this determination to achieve whatever you set out to do—you
took that part-time job to pay off your student loan—
you get on and do whatever it takes without complaint.'
He smiled. 'And I love your gentleness. I just know that
when you're with me, I feel complete.'

She moved in closer to him, winding an arm around
his waist. His words thrilled her, filled her with exhil-
aration. 'I think I'm willing to do more than give us a
chance. I've finally discovered what it is to be truly in
love.'

He folded her to him, the arm around her shoulders drawing her close. 'That's exactly how I feel.' He
dropped a kiss lightly on her forehead. 'It's been great,
sharing the same house, living together, in a way. Do
you think we might do something to make it a more
permanent arrangement?'

'Permanent?' She hardly dared hope that he was saying what she wanted most of all. 'What do you mean?'

He wrapped his arms around her. 'I mean it's dawned
on me, over these last few weeks, that I've fallen hope-

lessly in love with you, and I can't imagine how life would be without you... And I'd do anything to make sure that we can be together for always.'

She pulled in a shaky breath. 'I'd like that.' Her eyes shimmered with happiness. 'I'd really like that.' She could see the love in his eyes and feel the warmth of his body close to hers. It was a moment that would be seared into her brain for evermore. 'I love you,' she said.

'And I love you...so much that it hurts.' He dragged in a shaky breath. 'Will you marry me?'

'Yes, please.'

They grinned at each other. Then he drew her more closely to him and kissed her long and hard, until her senses began to swim and her heart swelled with the simple joy of being with him.

A few minutes later they came up for air. Jade was breathless, her body tingling with excitement, her spirits soaring.

'We have some celebrating to do,' he said.

'Maybe we should start with steak and a bottle of red wine...'

'Oh, yes. And lots of kisses to seal the bargain...'

'Sounds good to me.'

He kissed her again, and they were both laughing, joyous, lifted on a tide of elation. 'Shall we make it an August wedding?' he suggested, nuzzling at the creamy slope of her throat. 'We've so much to look forward to, you and I. Being together, buying a house that we can call our own.' He mused on that for a moment. 'I suppose it will have to be somewhere halfway between your family's home and mine.'

'I love you for saying that,' she said on a ragged sigh, lifting her face to him so that he could rain kisses over her cheeks and nose and mouth. She couldn't get enough of him.

Then, after a while, she asked, 'Do you really think we'll be able to afford a house, with London prices as they are?'

'I don't see why not. On my salary we'll perhaps have to settle for something tiny, or a flat, but anyway, by the time we're married, you'll be on your way to being a junior doctor, with a salary of your own, so perhaps between us we'll be able to afford something better.'

She laughed. 'You seem very sure I'll pass my exams and assessments.'

'I know you will. You'll be a terrific doctor, Jade. Anyway, we should manage to find some place to live that we both like. As long as we're together, what does it matter?'

He smiled. 'I can just see the cartoon for the magazine in my mind's eye... Who cares about exams? They're over and done with and we don't have a care in the world. You, me and Freddie are all bundled into the wedding car with tin cans tied to the back, and the caption says, "Three can live as cheaply as one."'

She laughed. 'You're very good with those cartoons. I'm sure that'll go down really well.'

'Yeah.' His gaze drifted over her. 'I can't wait to have you all to myself.'

'Same here.' She snuggled up to him.

'Together,' he murmured, 'we'll make a wonderful

team, both at work and in our home life. Things will turn out well for us. I know it.'

'I think so, too,' she said softly.

She wound her arms around his neck and drew his head down to her, and with the moonlight casting its blessing over them they sealed their future with a kiss.

* * * * *

Mills & Boon® Hardback

January 2012

ROMANCE

The Man Who Risked It All	Michelle Reid
The Sheikh's Undoing	Sharon Kendrick
The End of her Innocence	Sara Craven
The Talk of Hollywood	Carole Mortimer
Secrets of Castillo del Arco	Trish Morey
Hajar's Hidden Legacy	Maisey Yates
Untouched by His Diamonds	Lucy Ellis
The Secret Sinclair	Cathy Williams
First Time Lucky?	Natalie Anderson
Say It With Diamonds	Lucy King
Master of the Outback	Margaret Way
The Reluctant Princess	Raye Morgan
Daring to Date the Boss	Barbara Wallace
Their Miracle Twins	Nikki Logan
Runaway Bride	Barbara Hannay
We'll Always Have Paris	Jessica Hart
Heart Surgeon, Hero...Husband?	Susan Carlisle
Doctor's Guide to Dating in the Jungle	Tina Beckett

HISTORICAL

The Mysterious Lord Marlowe	Anne Herries
Marrying the Royal Marine	Carla Kelly
A Most Unladylike Adventure	Elizabeth Beacon
Seduced by Her Highland Warrior	Michelle Willingham

MEDICAL

The Boss She Can't Resist	Lucy Clark
Dr Langley: Protector or Playboy?	Joanna Neil
Daredevil and Dr Kate	Leah Martyn
Spring Proposal in Swallowbrook	Abigail Gordon

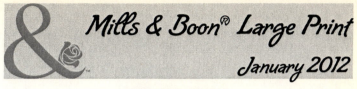

Mills & Boon® Large Print

January 2012

ROMANCE

The Kanellis Scandal	Michelle Reid
Monarch of the Sands	Sharon Kendrick
One Night in the Orient	Robyn Donald
His Poor Little Rich Girl	Melanie Milburne
From Daredevil to Devoted Daddy	Barbara McMahon
Little Cowgirl Needs a Mum	Patricia Thayer
To Wed a Rancher	Myrna Mackenzie
The Secret Princess	Jessica Hart

HISTORICAL

Seduced by the Scoundrel	Louise Allen
Unmasking the Duke's Mistress	Margaret McPhee
To Catch a Husband...	Sarah Mallory
The Highlander's Redemption	Marguerite Kaye

MEDICAL

The Playboy of Harley Street	Anne Fraser
Doctor on the Red Carpet	Anne Fraser
Just One Last Night...	Amy Andrews
Suddenly Single Sophie	Leonie Knight
The Doctor & the Runaway Heiress	Marion Lennox
The Surgeon She Never Forgot	Melanie Milburne

Mills & Boon® Hardback

February 2012

ROMANCE

An Offer She Can't Refuse	Emma Darcy
An Indecent Proposition	Carol Marinelli
A Night of Living Dangerously	Jennie Lucas
A Devilishly Dark Deal	Maggie Cox
Marriage Behind the Façade	Lynn Raye Harris
Forbidden to His Touch	Natasha Tate
Back in the Lion's Den	Elizabeth Power
Running From the Storm	Lee Wilkinson
Innocent 'til Proven Otherwise	Amy Andrews
Dancing with Danger	Fiona Harper
The Cop, the Puppy and Me	Cara Colter
Back in the Soldier's Arms	Soraya Lane
Invitation to the Prince's Palace	Jennie Adams
Miss Prim and the Billionaire	Lucy Gordon
The Shameless Life of Ruiz Acosta	Susan Stephens
Who Wants To Marry a Millionaire?	Nicola Marsh
Sydney Harbour Hospital: Lily's Scandal	Marion Lennox
Sydney Harbour Hospital: Zoe's Baby	Alison Roberts

HISTORICAL

The Scandalous Lord Lanchester	Anne Herries
His Compromised Countess	Deborah Hale
Destitute On His Doorstep	Helen Dickson
The Dragon and the Pearl	Jeannie Lin

MEDICAL

Gina's Little Secret	Jennifer Taylor
Taming the Lone Doc's Heart	Lucy Clark
The Runaway Nurse	Dianne Drake
The Baby Who Saved Dr Cynical	Connie Cox

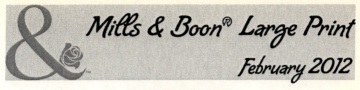

Mills & Boon® Large Print

February 2012

ROMANCE

The Most Coveted Prize	Penny Jordan
The Costarella Conquest	Emma Darcy
The Night that Changed Everything	Anne McAllister
Craving the Forbidden	India Grey
Her Italian Soldier	Rebecca Winters
The Lonesome Rancher	Patricia Thayer
Nikki and the Lone Wolf	Marion Lennox
Mardie and the City Surgeon	Marion Lennox

HISTORICAL

Married to a Stranger	Louise Allen
A Dark and Brooding Gentleman	Margaret McPhee
Seducing Miss Lockwood	Helen Dickson
The Highlander's Return	Marguerite Kaye

MEDICAL

The Doctor's Reason to Stay	Dianne Drake
Career Girl in the Country	Fiona Lowe
Wedding on the Baby Ward	Lucy Clark
Special Care Baby Miracle	Lucy Clark
The Tortured Rebel	Alison Roberts
Dating Dr Delicious	Laura Iding